Verity Landon was born in 1985 in Surrey, where she has lived ever since. Soon after her birth, it became obvious to her parents that she had problems with her vision, but despite being registered visually impaired, she went to mainstream primary and secondary schools, where her love of writing soon became apparent. While still at school, she won two county competitions for short stories.

For Carol and Hugh Landon, Jody Kary Barry and Ros Reeve.

Verity Landon

STAINED GLASS WINDOW

AUSTIN MACAULEY PUBLISHERS™

LONDON · CAMBRIDGE · NEW YORK · SHARJAH

A CIP catalogue record for this title is available from the British Library.

ISBN 9781528926133 (Paperback)
ISBN 9781528926140 (E-Book)

www.austinmacauley.com

First Published (2019)
Austin Macauley Publishers Ltd
25 Canada Square
Canary Wharf
London
E14 5LQ

I'd like to thank Hugh and Carol Landon, who have always given me amazing parental support. My brothers, sister and whole family who have always been there for me.

Jody Katy Barry, who has always offered amazing friendship and gave me emotional and practical support through my school years.

All the staff at the Howard of Effingham School who made everything accessible for me.

Ros Reeve and Angela Baker, who were learning support assistants all through primary school.

Chapter 1

Miss Moore was going to kill me when she got back!

I stared hopelessly at the broad watch face, following the little shiny seconds hand as it ticked endlessly round. I'd never noticed before that it was possible to hear the noise it made, but now it was all I could hear through the thick silence of the room: *Tick, tick, tick.*

My head rested heavily on one hand and my elbow dug into the hard wood-effect table. The clean sheets of squared paper lay untouched; the sun coming through the dusty window gave me the feeling that they were glaring up at me. I shut the book and made myself look away. Equally unused was the pen lying beside it. I picked it up and started twisting it carelessly through a strand of hair. The ink cartridge was running out so I changed it. There were a few blunt pencils at the bottom of my pencil case and I sharpened them onto the floor, making each lead end in a sharp point.

What was Miss Moore going to say?

Again I pushed this thought out of my mind, but it was getting more and more difficult to avoid. It kept popping back into my head like a spring that wouldn't stay down. There wasn't much else to think about.

I didn't care! I couldn't care! This attitude was the only realistic one to take in the situation, because if I let myself see it in any other way it gave me that funny feeling in my stomach and a horrible prickle at the back of my eyes.

In front of me the white board was covered in green scribble. The harder I stared at it, the more blurry it became.

Back to the watch. There was nowhere else in the room where it was safe to focus. Bent backs over books; the ticking joined now by the scratching of pens on paper. Now they would be glancing up at the board, now back down to their work. It made me feel sick. Nearly 4 o'clock . Only a few minutes more. Only a few more minutes! At last the bell rang, drowning out the ticking. I joined the rowdy rush out of the classroom door and clattered with the crowd down the stairs and across the playground. The air was wonderfully cool on my face as I pushed through the noise. I kept my eyes on the ground so I wouldn't be accused of not responding if somebody I knew waved at me.

Then I heard David's voice behind me, 'Hey Louise, wait!'

We usually had a bit of a chat before we separated to go home if we hadn't been in the last lesson together, but today it wouldn't be safe to stop. I'd have to ring him tonight and try to explain.

Somewhere amongst the noise I heard him call goodbye. I croaked back over my shoulder, but he couldn't possibly have heard me. Talking too loudly could be dangerous. I tried to walk a bit faster, pushing my way through a sea of schoolbags and bodies. I was nearly at breaking point. I must shut out the thoughts – just for a bit longer. Only about 15 minutes and I'd be home.

I groaned as I came round the corner of the Geography block. Naomi's unmistakable laughter was coming from the group around the bus stop. It sounded like water glugging down a drain. So the bus hadn't arrived yet! I sometimes talked to Naomi on the way home, but today I was so quiet that I doubt she even noticed me. Not that I minded.

I had to put up with more dragging minutes until the bus turned up. There were loads of people chatting around me over the thrum of the engine. Some of them were making plans for the evening and weekend, or talking about new clothes or CDs they'd bought. What if they knew how I was feeling?

Now here I was, as usual, in a big heap on my bed after angrily sweeping all the clothes and stuff off it onto the floor. At last I was home and it was safe; I could let go.

I sat there with my shoes kicked off against the door, cross-legged, facing away from the window, waiting for the tears to come. I let them run down my face, warm and salty on my tongue and, in a weird way, comforting. This was what I'd been waiting for. The frustrated anger flowed out with them in little gasps and sobs, sounding like a baby whimpering. I allowed the feelings that I'd desperately been trying to fight for the past hour to flood over me, letting the events play through my mind, scene by scene, like a terrible film. It was one that I'd seen loads of times before. You'd think I'd be bored with it by now.

It had already been one of those days. You know the kind; where every lesson lasts longer than the one before and you're wondering if all the clocks are slow. All the work seemed especially difficult, simply to spite me. I'd just been freed from an impossible Physics lesson. At least at that time I'd been sitting next to David, which made things a bit more bearable. I liked doing practical work with him because it usually went wrong. Like the time when we'd managed to blow up a test tube because we'd mixed the wrong chemicals or something.

I smiled through my tears at the thought of how I'd screamed in horror as the test tube burst in front of me and we'd both jumped back, and how, when we realised everyone in the class was looking at us, we'd cringed and then just cracked up.

I hated maths at the best of times, but the heat of the muggy Friday afternoon had made me extra knackered. I hoped the work wouldn't be too strenuous. Miss Moore was an OK teacher. Once, just before the summer holidays, she'd even let us make paper fans because it had been far too hot to do any work. Maybe it would be the same today if enough people made a fuss.

It was funny, I thought, that I'd ended up doing no work at all. In any other situation it would have been a god-send.

As I came through the door of the classroom I heard an unfamiliar voice coming from the figure sitting at the teacher's desk. It sounded croaky and old. A cover teacher! I groaned inside and any hopes of fan-making were shot to pieces. I could already tell that it would probably be a whole hour of intense maths problems in near silence. I wouldn't even have David to whisper to. I sighed too loudly as I dropped down on the chair at my desk in the front and braced myself for the boring ordeal which my already dozy brain was about to go through.

The bright sun that streamed in through the window seemed to bounce off the teacher's head. He must be bald! He was wearing dark blue; probably a suit. I wondered how he could bear to wear a jacket on a day like this. I rolled up my shirt sleeves, envying the students in those American schools where you were allowed to wear what you wanted. My tights were itchy against my legs and my skirt felt heavy and damp from sweat. It was really strange weather for September and I wished it was still the summer holidays. I suddenly thought that perhaps teachers didn't feel the heat. I grinned to myself. Maybe they didn't feel anything!

'All right everyone,' said Mr Baldy in a mechanical sort of voice as the last few people drifted in. I recognised the voice from somewhere, but what was his real name? I hoped he knew who I was. He started to write on the white board. There was a folder thick with paper on the desk in front of him. He must be copying from that. He was using one of those really annoying squeaky pens, adding to the irritation caused by the fly or wasp that was buzzing around the room. I frowned up at the board and the sunlight on it danced back, mocking me. The lines of work in faint scrawny handwriting were packed tightly together, covering most of the top half of the board.

I could hear a few people whinging around me, echoing my feeling. Mr Baldy looked down again, realising that the room had gone quiet; everyone waiting for him to give instructions. 'It says here that you have to do as much as possible in this lesson and finish the rest for homework.'

Oh how kind! The whining started up again but this time louder. I thought about all the Chemistry coursework that had to be in for tomorrow and regretted having put it off. He sat down at the desk, and I waited for him to give me the sheet he'd been copying from. Surely he felt sorry for us; glad he wasn't expected to do all this? Dad was always going on about how the work had got easier since he was at school. I bet he'd never had this much homework. Yes, I'd put that to him tonight. That's if I survived the lesson in this greenhouse. Why hadn't Mr. Baldy given me the sheets yet? I willed him to find the message that Miss Moore would have written about me and my 'special requirements'.

Now he was rumbling on about how he expected 'silent hard work' and 'no bother because he had a lot of marking to do.' We were allowed a five minute break in the middle of the lesson if we 'behaved ourselves'. Five whole minutes? Huh!

Where were my papers? I tried to focus my eyes on the teacher. Alongside the folder there was now a pile of green that must be exercise books and what I guessed was some sort of personal organiser, but the folder with the sheets of work in it seemed to be closed. I started wishing more than ever that this was a normal lesson.

I looked back at the white board. It was so close that I almost had to tilt my head backwards, but the words and numbers were still just scribbles. I held onto the red plastic chair with a tight fist, like a toddler about to throw a tantrum. My right arm was stretched out across the table towards the teacher's desk. Again there was only the scratching sound of pens. He must have started doing his marking, and obviously had nothing more to say. Slowly I drew the arm back towards me, realising, with a bit of a jolt, that if I wanted my sheets I was going to have to ask for them and admit my weakness.

That's when panic began to set in; when it really hit me that I was on my own. I looked despairingly at the empty chair next to me. Why was I so crap at maths? If I was in the same group as David, he could secretly whisper everything on the board for me to write down in the back of my book. Now there was lots of sighing and more pen scratching as the rest of the class copied the questions into their books and then the room fell heavy with silence as well as with heat. Craig made some comment about how pointless pi was unless you could eat it. My head turned towards him and I couldn't suppress a little smile. There was that distinctive voice! Richer than all the other voices! The teacher gave a sharp 'Sshh', which made me jump. Oh great! I'd drawn attention to myself and he must've seen that I wasn't doing anything. I supposed he must have wondered why I hadn't even opened my book yet.

'Is there a problem?'

He must be looking right at me now. This was my chance. I felt the words in my mouth and heard them shouting in my head, 'I can't see the work on the board and I need the sheets you copied from.' I even got as far as opening my mouth, but then closed it again. I probably looked like a fish and I knew I was going red. The teacher realised that I wasn't going to say anything,

'Get on with it then please.' And he gestured to the squiggles with a wide wave of his arm.

I strained my eyes ahead, feeling the frustration gripping me. If only I was just a few inches closer, but then my nose would almost be touching the board. All I needed was that sheet; all I needed to do to get it was ask. Sounds easy, doesn't it? From time to time the others would all be looking up. I knew that even those at the back could do it. As if by magic, they knew what was on the board and down into their books it went. I hated them! I hated everyone!

And then the real anger kicked into gear. That same old, 'why can't I just see it anyway?!' Everyone else can! They took it for granted. I felt like slapping them all and their 'normality' and putting them in my shoes and making them hurt like I was hurting! I could feel my face and my insides screwing up. I probably had those ugly lines down my forehead that you get when you're frowning. I wanted to scream really loudly and let it ring around the stupid silent room.

Right at the back of my mind I was angry with myself for being such a baby and not facing up to things. I'd been in this situation long enough; almost since I was born. Yes! I hated myself much more than the others. I pinched my arm really hard under the table until it made me let out a little gasp. There was the sound of movement at the teacher's desk. Had he heard my pathetic yelp? I looked away and leaned over my book. He became quiet, apparently satisfied that I was working.

The white board blurred even more as my unworthy eyes filled up. I blinked rapidly. They didn't have the right to cry! It's then that I gave in and sat in silence for the rest of the hour. How was I going to explain to Miss Moore something that I didn't understand myself? I sniffed loudly and then cleared my throat to make it seem like I had a cold. I was getting dangerously near breaking point.

So that was when I had had to stop thinking about it, and wait until I got home. I had spent the rest of the lesson staring at my enormous watch and counting down the seconds and minutes.

Chapter 2

It took longer than usual for the crying to stop completely. I didn't feel better. I had a bunged-up nose and a headache, and now I felt even more tired. Replaying the same thing over and over again does get tiring after a while. I lay pathetically on my bed, listening to my breath, which was deep and irregular: rising and falling really loudly in my ears. I hit the sky-blue wall beside me with my fist. My knuckles throbbed and I wished I hadn't done it. What an idiot! Here we go again!

How stupid was I? I was angry about something that I'd brought on myself. How easy it should be just to ask for help, and I didn't know why I couldn't do it. But I was well acquainted with the physical feeling of sickness and embarrassment that came at the prospect of it. It must be clear by now that events like this were fairly regular. Anyone would have thought I enjoyed it, because logically I knew it was totally unnecessary, but it only took a few misplaced sheets of paper to make me erupt.

The sun was just starting to go down over the rooftops outside the window as the next stage of my thunderstorm started; Guilt! In came all the millions of people with legitimate reasons for feeling the way I did. All the stuff that was constantly on the news (which Dad watched every day and I did my best to ignore.) People starving to death on other continents or being wrongly accused of crimes and living in prison for years. And all I was miserable about was not being able to read some writing for a subject that I didn't even care about anyway. I had everything I needed. You'd think I was in the 'bereaved' or 'treated badly as a child' bracket.

It was as if I'd suddenly developed some kind of illness. A visual problem which really hadn't bothered me and which most of the time I forgot about had become the subject of so many of my thoughts and the majority of my upsets. There's no way to describe how terrible it felt to be in a room full of people who all had a privilege that I didn't. And one that they didn't even appreciate! I gritted my teeth and screamed in my head.

'Hello?'

'Hi Dave it's me.'

My voice was still a bit shaky as I spoke, but I'd just about managed to pull myself together and besides I was starting to get hungry. I'd been standing by the phone for ages, trying to think of somebody in my maths class whose number I knew. But there was no one. And even if there had been they'd have asked why I didn't know the work from class today and I obviously wouldn't have been able to explain.

'Louise! How are you? I hope you're not in a mood with me. You looked really annoyed about something after school today.'

I felt a bit guilty.

'No Dave, it's not you.....'

'Good.' He paused, 'Well, what's up then?'

'Oh, y'know, I was just a bit tired and fed up with school.'

'Come on, there was obviously more to it than that. You looked as if you were about to cry.'

Although I was closer to David than any of my other friends, and he tried his best to understand, I couldn't share all this with anyone; not even him. Once when we'd been walking down Haslecombe High Street chatting about something – laughing and all that – he'd suddenly jabbed me in the ribs and whispered, 'Look who it is!' and pointed across the street. It had turned out to be Becky Myres, who he fancied, but didn't have the guts to ask out. A bit like me and Craig I suppose (although the thought of asking Craig out in this lifetime just made me laugh.) We'd had a little chat with her and then carried on, but I wasn't happy. How useless was I not to be able to recognise somebody just across the street? I hadn't said anything to David. It didn't matter all day and then I'd had my sob session that night as I kept going over the thought of following his finger with my gaze and the frustration of seeing a mass of figures moving on the other side of the road. I knew if I'd talked it out with him things would've been better. But I couldn't talk about it. Even thinking about my eyes was painful. The fantasy where it only existed in my bedroom was the only option; to pretend it wasn't real until I was forced to remember that it was, cry for a while on my bed, then forget it again. That was how it was, and the only way it could be.

I sat down on the chair in the hall.

'What's wrong?'

I hesitated. 'Stuff's just getting on top of me at the moment. Y'know, too much work.'

He tutted in sympathy.

'I know what you mean.' He'd obviously been debating whether or not to add the next part, because there was a bit of an awkward silence before he spoke. 'Mind you.... things might be... harder for you.'

I felt my cheeks go red even though he couldn't see me.

'What do you mean by that?'

'I don't know.... Reading and stuff... You might get more... tired.' He could tell that he'd said the wrong thing.

'Got any plans for the weekend?' he asked. That was one consolation. At least I didn't have to face school again for a couple of days.

'I've got some free tickets to go ice skating, do you wanna come?' I could tell from the cautious way he said this that he didn't know whether it was an acceptable thing to ask. For a couple of seconds the image of the rink through the glass at the Leisure Centre flashed into my mind, with all the people whizzing around in all directions; but I reminded myself my sight problem didn't exist in the daytime, so it would be fine.

By the end of the evening I'd managed to shut out the events of the day, immune at least for a few hours. Whilst we were watching TV Mark pointed out something funny, and I was sitting at the other end of the room eating dinner. True to form I laughed anyway, and added to the false impression he had of my visual problem – it was my own fault if my abilities were over-estimated. In bed that night there might be a couple of tears. Tonight it would be the 'why me and not my brother' category. It could just have easily have happened to Mark. But it wouldn't last long. This aspect of the subject had had a lot of attention in these sessions before and I was exhausted.

Chapter 3

Next day I persuaded Mum to drop me off at the station on her way to work so I could meet David and go into town with him. I had to get up ridiculously early because she had to be there for nine. David did a paper round anyway so it didn't matter to him. He didn't understand about lie-ins. He used to phone me at half past eight on Saturdays until I'd put him straight. Getting up for school was quite enough for me. I loved my bed in the mornings, even though it was in that bedroom where I sat and cried almost every evening.

David was always the one in charge of us getting around. Perhaps that's always the way it is in friendships anyway. He bought the tickets, he knew when the next train was, he knew which direction to take. I felt uneasy thinking about what days-out would be like without him. I'd never had to manage on my own, and if I ever tried to travel anywhere, there'd be a world of asking, 'What platform?' 'Which way?' Which station?' I wasn't sure whether David was aware that I was totally taking his lead and I let myself pretend I wasn't, but in truth, I was terrified of what my future would be like, and I would probably have a fret about it tonight. But I'd decided that today was going to be a good day. We were going to the ice-rink.__

'Look at them! They're going so fast! What if I get in someone's way?'

'You don't have to go in the middle.'

Everyone seemed to be whizzing by effortlessly and at great speed.

I couldn't understand how people managed to stay upright.

'Look. Loads of people are going round holding the side. See? There's a big group that's gonna come in front of you in a sec.'

They skidded past us and fell over in a bundle, shrieking with laughter and I smiled with relief. If other people were allowed to look stupid doing this then I was too. David braved it first. We'd staggered to the entrance in our massive boots. It was how I imagined walking on the moon might be. He stepped on to the ice, his hand gripping the bar at the edge. He held the other one out to me and I swerved uncertainly into him, making him shout, 'Hold the bar at the side, not me!' We too ended up in a heap in fits of laughter. My jeans were soaked, that was all, but I hoped no-one would think I'd wet myself!

'I haven't fallen over like that since I was about six,' David said When I was six I used to spend my life falling over.

Skating soon became easier as my feet grew accustomed to the speed of the ground moving underneath them and I found I was leaving David behind.

'You're way better than me! Have you been before?' he said, when I stopped to let him catch up.

'No. And I'm not way better than you.' Although I knew I was! At each end of the rink there was an opening for people to get on and off the ice and we had to skate along it with nothing to hold on to. I was unsteady but David was worse, although I didn't have the heart to tell him. He would wobble nervously with his arms all over the place. Skating wasn't half as hard as I'd expected. Although the ice moved too easily under my feet I seemed to be becoming more and more used to it.

Someone came from the middle where the better skaters were. They seemed to bring one foot in front of the other and glide along on each in turn. I could see myself doing that....

It was just a thought at first. The figures in the centre were moving faster than those around the edges. Suddenly my decision was made. Even though I was shy and I thought I was stupid, I was determined. There'd be no harm in trying! I stopped suddenly and David swerved in next to me, grabbing my shoulder and almost pulling us both down.

'Louise! You could've warned me that you were going to stop!'

'Sorry.'

'How'd you get so good so quickly?' I looked away to hide a grin.

'I'm goin' in,' I said in a phoney American accent and pointed to the middle of the rink. He seemed horrified as if it was some kind of battlefield.

'Do you want me to come with you?' Did he really think I needed his help? I put him straight on that.

'Not if you don't want to.' I sensed his relief. I noted he was wearing a bright red T shirt and blue jeans. That was reassuring. He'd be easily noticeable. As soon as I'd let go and skated a couple of metres, somebody whooshed past and I was down on the ice.

'Sorry,' they called, 'but watch where you're going!'

off again. I'd already made up my mind that I was going to be good at this. I was better than a few of the others around me I noticed as I saw that some, like David, were glued to the edge. I was gaining a bit of speed now; just enough so that the air felt cool on my face and through my hair. I bumped into a few people but everyone was doing that.

At least, I let myself believe that they were.

I didn't want to be away from David for too long. It would be mean of me to leave him clinging to the edge on his own, so I decided to come to the rink alone sometime soon. I liked skating already. It made me feel good about myself, and what else did that? I looked around the rink for the red T shirt. Naturally I checked the sides first, trying in vain to sweep them with my eyes. No joy! I had to resort to going around the whole circuit until I found him. When I did he was waving his arms at me, in huge circles like a windmill. I felt a bit flustered but said nothing as usual and actually forgot about it instead of saving the hurt for later. He drew me towards him so that his face was almost touching my ear and pointed across to the far side of the ice. 'Look,' he said, and I peered towards the figures. 'What?' I growled. I frowned; he should know better than to do this. But did he have any reason to know better?

He turned to face me, as if suddenly remembering that I couldn't 'look.' It seemed strange that he should forget about it. I never did.

'It's that boy you fancy.' We were so close that I could see that David was grinning.

Did he mean Craig? The god-of-the-maths-class Craig? The drop-dead-gorgeous-but-way-out-of-my-league Craig? I'd told

David about him in exchange for his story about Becky Myres who sat next to us in History. Craig had only joined the school in the middle of last term and I hadn't really discovered him for a couple of weeks. He was the only thing that made maths bearable. Of course I didn't know him at all. He was quite cheeky to the teacher – really funny – and he had the admiration of the whole class already. He'd also managed to make it so that it was an honour to be his friend. I knew half the girls in my year fancied him and there were loads of far cooler, not to mention prettier, girls than me. But I could dream couldn't I?

'What? He's here?'

'Don't drool so much or you'll melt the ice.'

'You'd better not be having me on.' I'd forgotten that usually I'd just say 'oh yeah' and pretend I could see Craig.

'He's over there with some other blokes, I swear.'

I gazed intently at my reflection in the glass barrier at the edge of the rink where we were standing. I looked awful! David patted his blond spiky hair in imitation. I gave him a look and then squinted over at the distant figures on the other side, one of whom must be Craig. They all moved quickly and easily. Suddenly I let out a shrill girlie giggle, which I was to regret because David kept mimicking it for weeks afterwards. I'd realised that if Craig was here on the ice then he might be into skating. And I'd become OK at it so quickly! People tend to like those who share their interests don't they?

'Is he a good skater?'

'He's showing off in my opinion. Keeps doing these little twirly things where you turn round and go into the air a bit.' He used his hands to help me to picture it.

'Impressive and at the same time showing his strength and fitness,' I thought. So Craig must be good at skating. One of the best here, according to David's description. This was certainly an incentive `for me to improve!

I'd often dream about what it would be like to be that privileged girl who was going out with Craig. I knew that I'd immediately acquire loads of friends. During his short time at our school he'd already gained a reputation with the staff. He was a bit of a class clown and I suppose that added to his appeal. There was a little group that he hung around with. He was particularly friendly with one girl called Kate and it goes without saying that I, along with loads of the rest of the female population, was jealous of her. He was really nice to those in his exclusive little group. His friendly personality went, in my mind, with his good looks. I didn't want to believe that in reality he might be one of those mega ego blokes. He certainly appeared to be, from the way he treated the teachers and occasionally combed his hair in class, but I had invented an image of him as I wanted him to be. My eyes prevented me from even having a clear knowledge of what he looked like. So it was the tanned complexion and the huge eyes that I'd created which made me melt. One day I might get close to him and realise that actually they looked like little lumps of coal and be disappointed. But of course I knew that the chances of me ever realistically being his girlfriend were similar to those of me passing my maths GCSE.

I really hated my shyness and reluctance to talk to people. I'd never spoken a word to Craig in my life, except for that time when Miss Moore made him sit next to me at the front because he was mucking about too much at the back. She set it as a punishment, but you can imagine how I felt about it. He borrowed my calculator, and for ages I'd go over the way he'd said, 'Can I borrow your calculator?' How he'd been talking to me and nobody else! That supposedly inanimate and widely hated object was now among my prized possessions. Maths classes aren't the best situations to meet people. How could I expect him, the master of cool, to go out with me, the stupid kid with the squint?

The subject of Craig was dropped, and David and I continued to skate around, and fall over – well, he did anyway – but the image of Craig's move on the ice wouldn't remove itself from my mind. It stayed with me all day. It's amazing how I'd managed to go from being so unhappy yesterday to being almost ecstatic today. 'Ridiculously fickle' as my Gran had once said when I was little and I'd been disappointed with one of my presents at Christmas, but straight afterwards received the desired dolls' house and been immediately transported to seventh heaven.

Several times that afternoon my only response to David's comments would be 'mmm'. It was Craig I could see in front of me. I was skating into his arms; he was carrying me above his head like in ice ballets. {I'd magically lost about a stone of course}. We skated apart in graceful circles, which got smaller and smaller until we met. He looked into my eyes with deep admiration. Of course they didn't have the squint. They were perfect! It was perfect!

I lay in bed that night, the curtains drawn with just a crack between them, which allowed a shaft of light to come in and cast shadows all over the room, either from the moon or from a street lamp. For the first time in ages I wasn't miserable and I wasn't in tears. I had it all mapped out. I'd get really good at skating. I'd practise hard and buy an expensive pair of skates – be a real enthusiast like Craig seemed to be. I'd see him on the ice one Saturday morning, skate casually over and do one of his twirly things a couple of metres away from him so that it didn't look as if I was trying to impress. He'd congratulate me in that wonderful voice. He'd be really amazed and then he'd ask me to be part of his little group and we'd all skate together.

I'd be one of them.

Chapter 4

Second period on Wednesday was when my next maths lesson was going to be. Needless to say I was dreading it. We'd have to hand our books in at the end and Miss Moore would see that I hadn't done any of the work she'd set. She'd ask why and I would obviously lie and she'd make judgements about my personality that weren't true. She'd think I was getting lazy and maybe I'd move down a set; then I wouldn't be with Craig. I pretended to myself I didn't care. It was the easiest option, if not the most sensible.

However, next Wednesday I didn't go to school at all. I didn't pretend I was ill, although I'd considered it, but I'd forgotten I had a hospital appointment in London. It was an annual thing – just to check that everything was OK with my eyes. Usually it was in the morning, and Mum took time off work and she and I would make a day of it. I used to like going to places like Hamley's, but now I preferred Oxford Street or Camden Town for a bit of 'retail therapy.'

I don't know what it is about London that makes me get excited. It isn't far away. Only about 50 miles up the motorway from Haslecombe. I'd always loved it when I was little. All the noise and smells and things to do. But a visit was still a treat for me. Some people think it's a special occasion to go to the seaside, and I'm there nearly every day so it's quite ordinary.

We caught the train and then the tube to the hospital – Mum had never been much of a traffic driver – but she used the excuse that it was more 'environmentally friendly' than going by car. I thought about the excitement I used to feel when we got on the train. I would look at the commuters reading their papers and hugging their brief cases. They all seemed really bored. I wondered if they liked their jobs; what it was they were going to do at work. Today one man, sitting next to us, was wearing his glasses low on his face and even I could see his eyes over the rims. I decided he was a lawyer.

Although I was looking forward to London I knew that once again this would be one of those occasions when I would have to face up to things. They'd make me read eye charts and I'd only be able to see the top letter. It would bring home how disadvantaged I really was and my little shell would be shattered. '15 percent' would scream at me from everywhere.

As I entered the waiting room I remembered, with a familiar sinking feeling, that I was one of the luckier ones here.

There had been a time years ago when I hadn't known that I was any different from anybody else. I thought that everybody could see like me. Of course I knew that I had an 'eye problem' but I now realised how careful my parents had been to look after me. There had been one particular and memorable moment though, when I'd realised that I actually couldn't see like everybody else. It had been while we were on holiday. Nowadays I enjoyed holidays and music and times when I wasn't forced to face things; times which allowed me to forget. You meet loads of people on holiday who don't know you and you can just be who you are and nobody knows. On this particular holiday Mark and I had decided to secretly buy an ice cream with our pocket money. We'd gone to an ice cream van and Mark had suddenly said 'let's get out of here! Mum and Dad are watching!' I couldn't see them anywhere! This is where that spiral had begun.

We sat down in the big airy waiting room with fairly comfortable chairs all around it and walls of a nice spring green. A bit different from the white walls and hard chairs of my earliest memories. As soon as I'd looked around and caught snippets of various conversations I began to feel the surge of guilt which I only allowed myself to feel when I was here. I was one of the lucky ones. A little boy sat in one corner asking his mum if there were many people in the room. A bent-backed old lady sat next to him holding her white stick. A girl, who sounded as if she was about my age, was wearing dark glasses, which I guessed were to disguise an artificial eye. I momentarily frowned on all my self-pity. Nearly everyone here had suffered far more than I had. Only the other day I'd cried just because I couldn't see some writing. There'd been an option that would've allowed me to be able to see it. I would've only had to ask but I hadn't taken it, because I was too stubborn. Some of the people here couldn't see at all. I shut my eyes and let the darkness engulf me and imagined living in that world forever. No colour, no beautiful sights like sunsets. No hope of ever recognising anybody, no matter how bright their clothes were. They only had the voice recognition option.

I picked up a leaflet that lay on a table beside me; anything to take my mind off the situation. I was used to only being able to look at the pictures and read the captions in leaflets but this one was in really large print. 'About Retinoblastoma' it said. It made me feel sick just reading that word. It means 'cancer of the retina.'

I read on to find that one in 20,000 babies suffers from it. I smiled. Ironic really; proof that I really was "special", but I'd have settled for 'ordinary' any day. Imagine being in the "Ordinary Needs" group!

'The bilateral type can be inherited or develop spontaneously.' That was typical too. None of my family had it. Only me. What was it Mark had said this morning? That it wasn't fair and I was lucky to miss school? He was right, it wasn't fair!

Then my name was called and I went into a room with 'Retinoblastoma Clinic' written in big white letters on a black background over the door. I looked furiously at the words.

It had all started ages ago. I'd only been three months old when it was found. Not old enough to understand like I did now. I'd been through the motions – radiotherapy, laser treatment, a cobalt disc. Oh, I knew all the words! And it was all over now, apart from the fact that I was left with limited vision. It had all happened too long ago for me to know what it was like to see properly.

I often wonder why hospitals always have that smell. Is it a special spray they buy to make it feel more like a hospital? We walked down the glossy corridors and the occasional nurse walked past with one of those big trolleys with loads of boxes on it that must be full of instruments. What were they all for? Our feet made that creaky noise on the floor as we walked. It looked shiny and sticky even though it wasn't. Why are hospital floors always like that?

'How are you Louise?'

A short woman with dark curly hair and a white coat had sat me down in the huge white room with a high ceiling and black blinds. They must get those coats dirty easily. 'And they're intimidating `I thought 'It makes you think that you're mentally ill and they're going to take you away.' Suddenly I wondered what it would be like to be mentally ill. That could happen to anyone too.

'Fine.'

She usually had a bit of a chat with me. She'd known me since I was born. It was natural to lie. It wasn't worth telling her about all the ordeals.

'Are you coping with your eyes at the moment?'

'Yeah, I'm doing OK.' I felt the warmth in my cheeks.

'I thought that now you're a bit older, we might talk about the future a bit.' The future? What was there to say except that it looked bleak? No independence, no driving........ As usual guilt had only lasted for a few minutes. Now it was replaced with the old familiar self-pity. All my friends would be buying cars and learning to drive in a few years and I'd be stuck with the public transport. It wasn't fair! The anger was beginning to rise again. Those thoughts must stop for now.

'We could arrange for you to have mobility training to help you get around.' This, in my opinion would just be putting salt in the wound.

'Yes, that's a great idea, isn't it Louise?'

Mum jumped in before I had the chance to stop her. I glowered at her across the room.

'And we could look into cosmetic surgery to straighten the squint perhaps.'

I brightened somewhat. We'd discussed it last year, but I hadn't known that it was a definite possibility. The fact that I was cross-eyed caused me problems. When I looked in the mirror I always saw a terrible face looking back at me. In reality it probably wasn't that bad but, all the same, when people came up close they could see that something was the matter with my eyes. If they were straightened it would help me to pretend. Nobody would know. Nobody would even guess.

We went back into the waiting area and the guilt was switched on again. I momentarily resolved to be thankful for the sight I did have and never again to cry like a stupid baby about how unlucky I was. Of course it didn't last. Passionate as I was about it now with these people all around me, as soon as I left I would forget and go back into the world where it was only me who was unlucky and who had to bear any problems. I was the only one that mattered.

The Doctor, whom I had also known all my life, looked at the back of my eyes after I'd had eye drops to make my pupils dilate. I sat in a dark room whilst he shone a bright light into my stinging eyes. When I was little I used to hate that part. I would try and run away and screw up my eyes so that they couldn't put the drops in. They made them sting and my vision felt as if I'd just had a huge shock or woken up from deep sleep. I could actually taste the drops too.

'Everything's fine. We'll see you in a year'.

We went to Oxford Street and I bought a nice pair of trousers and shoes. I think Mum wanted to give me a bit of a present after going on the emotional roller coaster. We ate dinner in a small cafe on a street corner where a little band had set up. They'd probably only collected a couple of pence for a whole morning's work.

We went to see a Musical in the evening and I couldn't stop thinking of all the amazing singing actors. Singing well is something I really wished I could do. I could sing OK. It was one of those things that wasn't affected; that nobody could be better at because they could see.

It was great to hear an amazing Musical, but we could only afford seats at the back. I couldn't see anything that was going on on the stage. Everyone else could! My earlier thoughts of being lucky were shot to pieces.

Lying in bed that night I thought of Craig again. I was imagining him and me skating together and then he was holding me in his arms. Today was finally over and I could go back to how things really were. Forget Retinoblastoma! Why did they have to write a leaflet about it when it was so rare? Rare enough that it could be 'genetic' and none of the rest of my lucky family even had it! Genetic? My whole body suddenly felt cold. Did that mean that my children could inherit it from me?! I could potentially push everything that I'd been through onto the shoulders of an innocent child? Why hadn't I thought of this before?

I could see it now. A miniature me lying in bed crying just like me. Trying to comprehend all the complicated emotions, just like I had to. And why did they have to go through it all? Because I was their mother.

'Oh God,' I whispered.

I padded across the landing and knocked on Mum and Dad's door, just like I used to when I'd had a bad dream. They must be asleep. I could hear Dad snoring.

'Mum?' I whispered shakily through the darkness.

'What?' She sounded tired. It must have been a great emotional effort to help me have a bearable day today.

'Is it true that.....my eyes and all that could be inherited by my kids?'

There was silence. I wished I could see her face through the darkness. I willed her to say 'no' although I knew the answer already.

The light suddenly came on, making me jump. I moved over to her and sat down on the bed beside her. She put her hand on my shoulder. I could suddenly see that this was something she'd known she'd have to tell me for ages but had been waiting for the right moment, which hadn't come until now.

'There's a lot they can do these days, genetics and things..... things are much more hopeful than they used to be.........'

'But it's true though?'

She was silent for a moment and then put her arms around my shoulders.

'Yes.'

'No,' I whispered. 'No!'

Some things aren't necessary to get involved with. Sometimes there's nothing you can do to change something, but there is no way you can deny it. I knew that this wasn't my fault and it wasn't the time for me to be thinking about it. It must be put aside until I needed to deal with it. And that is what I did. I wouldn't allow myself to think about it again for years.

I did have to face that maths lesson next afternoon though. At least Craig would be there, and I could live through a detention. Today we had a morning assembly in the main hall. It was more important to be on time for school on assembly mornings. If I arrived after the bell on a normal day Mr. Campbell would let me off and mark me in anyway; he was one of my favourite teachers. But on these occasions the class would have already disappeared and I'd have to sneak in at the back and get a 'late detention.' I always got up with as little time to spare as possible, which, annoyingly was why I was usually late. David expected it nowadays and was actually surprised if I burst in on time. Mum ran me into school on her way to work so I would blame it on her. It was a good job she didn't expect me to catch the bus in the mornings as well as the afternoons because I know I'd have missed it.

This morning Mr. Campbell had just started calling the register when I erupted through the classroom door. Almost all the seats seemed filled already as usual. I wondered how they all managed it.

'Well done,' David whispered as I fell into my seat. I was tired out and I tried to disguise my heavy breathing by coughing. I'd only been running from the school car park. I was far too unfit.

I'd never been a great fan of assemblies, they were a waste of quarter of an hour, and you just had to sit and be moaned at or educated about something that really didn't interest anyone, by a teacher who seemed bored at what she had to say. Like how "a knowledge of maths and science is essential for your future". Filling you full of "facts", when they could be helping you how to think. Just as if everyone was exactly the same! That was today's topic and I'd switched off a couple of minutes into it, imagining a whole country full of robot children, all with the same programme. Most of the rest of the students had stopped listening too, by the sounds of the whispering all around me. I started picking at a loose thread on my jacket and pulling it. It got longer and longer and I wondered if the whole thing would unravel into one endless string if I pulled far enough. This was fifteen minutes of my life being taken up. That could add up to days or weeks or maybe even months out of a whole lifetime. Time that could be spent on holiday, writing a poem, learning a new skill or doing a parachute jump. I was distracted from these interesting thoughts by what Mrs. Eagle was saying. Our work experience placements had come. This was a week in which we had to visit a business or a shop or something, and get 'experience' of what it was like to be in the 'real world'. The thought of it made me shrivel up inside. We'd all had to fill in a form at the end of last term identifying our strengths and preferences. They'd been sent off and we would've been put into placements in different environments. I wondered nervously where mine would be.

I tried to recollect what I'd written on my form. I knew I'd said that I wanted to work with people, which I regretted now, as I thought about how many new hairstyles and voices I might have to get to know, and all the people I might be forced into polite conversations with. I'd also put that I was a 'good listener,' and I wondered where on earth that had come from. I'd probably end up in a telephone advertising service.

We were told to go to our form rooms at the end of the day to collect the papers showing our placements. I knew that I was going to spend the rest of the day with the anxiety chewing at my brain. I suppose there was a tiny bit of excitement mixed in with it somewhere. After all, I might end up in a chocolate factory or as a taste-tester for ice cream. Hmmm... and pigs might fly!

My wandering mind ventured back to what the Head of Year was saying. Not much; just the usual complaints about too much litter and bad conduct and forthcoming exams. Finally we were freed to go to our first lessons and I sighed as I wandered out of the door, remembering that mine was PE.

It's not that I don't like sports. Some can be really fun, like swimming and ice skating (as I'd found out last weekend). But in school I didn't think it was possible for sport to have any favourable qualities. For a start all the girls had to wear the most hideous skirts you can imagine for PE. They were navy blue and pleated and flared. Why didn't the teachers think it suitable for us to just wear a comfortable pair of trousers?

Then there were the games we had to play; a selection consisting of rounders and tennis in the summer and hockey and netball in the winter. All of these, you notice, are ball games. Full of the possibility of being hit in the face and, on an extra lucky day, some rain or strong winds would be thrown in. This had disastrous effects on even the best players, due to our skirt problems!

My unfitness was my own fault I suppose. Just a few metres made me out of breath. Sometimes, if the teacher was feeling really friendly, we would do cross country running up on the top field. I almost had my fingers crossed that this wouldn't be today's horrendous trauma.

We were put into single sex groups for PE, which meant I wasn't with David. The boys were allowed to play football. Not fair! All the girls thought football was far more fun than netball.

Abby and I had made friends through our similar feelings about PE. If ever we did practising in pairs we were the two that everyone else rejected so we went together. It was a good job the class didn't have an odd number or I would've had to partner the evil, unrelenting teacher, Mrs. Winship.

Abby wasn't an 'average' friend. Y'know, the kind who comes from a normal house and lives a normal life and the sort you have very normal light-hearted conversations with. First of all there was her appearance. She was tall and slim with long curly chestnut hair that reached almost to her waist, envied throughout the class. It always seemed to have that smooth shine, even at the end of the day or after a windy netball hour. I'd asked her what shampoo she used and I'd gone out and bought some. Of course it didn't work on my messy tangles.

I'd only been round her house a couple of times but it wasn't a house that you'd forget easily. Set back from the road down a little lane of its own. It was painted white, which made it more impressive at first glance, along with the stone lions that sat on the gate posts! Then there was the huge entrance hall with a staircase in the middle like the Von Trapp home in 'The Sound of Music.' And her room was huge. It even had its own sofa in the corner and a double bed.

Hanging around with Abby got a bit tedious sometimes. I didn't see her much out of school. It wasn't that she was a nasty person. Conversation just always seemed to centre round her and what she had or who she knew. I'd been on a shopping spree with her once – an experience never to be repeated.

'Hi Louise! Guess who?' As I dragged myself up the steps to the changing room, after waiting in the rain that had begun to spatter onto my head as if to spite me.

I saw her standing by the door.

'Hi.'

'What do you think of my new bag?'

It looked similar to one that I'd seen in London but couldn't afford. See my point? She was one of those people that you can only manage in small doses. She wasn't afraid to tell you about her luck. I don't think she meant to boast. She was trying to be nice, as I always had to tell myself. And when you knew her as well as I did, you started to benefit from her good luck. She wasn't particularly popular though. She was a hard worker and didn't get out much. A bit like me in that respect.

'I wonder where we've been placed.'

'Ooh, so do I! I said that I enjoy music. I hope I haven't been put in a CD shop!'

She had grade 5 on the piano and a really nice singing voice too. She'd had her voice trained a bit by a singing teacher and I sometimes wished that I could try that.

Mrs. Philips entered the changing room and I tutted without thinking. She was the 'support' teacher who came to help me in practical lessons like PE. I hated her like a toddler can hate a playgroup assistant. She made me stand out and look different. I expect I put her through hell in those lessons. I was always blunt and maybe even rude to her, just like a young kid would throw a tantrum if the adult with them was giving them the red cup instead of the blue one. I was surprised I hadn't been told off for it and that she'd never complained about me to my form teacher. She must have dreaded PE lessons almost as much as I did.

Abby nudged me in the ribs. I suppose she was being sympathetic but she still had that priceless bag! The one thing that she wasn't good at didn't matter to me anyway.

Mrs. Philips was coming towards me. Sometimes I was almost civil to her if I was in a good mood. She was probably wondering what to expect this lesson. Abuse from a stupid little kid with a chip on her shoulder or a co-operative human being? As usual a picture came into my head of her dressed in some kind of warrior's outfit, holding a shield, and me a huge green monster with googly eyes.

'Hello Louise.'

'Hi.'

'How are you?'

'OK.'

'We're doing netball today.'

I scowled and, in my usual baby way, didn't make any effort to hide my feelings.

'You don't have to play if you don't want to. You, Abby and I could go and do some practice out on the other field instead.'

I knew Abby was smiling at me. 'Great!' she was thinking, 'a chance to escape the hell.' And so was I, just for a few seconds, before I thought about what going off separately to practise entailed. The teachers knew that I wouldn't be much use in a netball game and so did my fellow students, as I sometimes heard them tell one another. Of course I would much rather not play. But, as usual, Mrs. Philips would 'supervise' as I did my best to run up and down the track in the field and Abby would 'lead' me. That wretched field with the running track where we would go was right next to the netball court where all the class could see us and my 'special needs' would be specifically displayed. Me, running along and a pretty girl running in front like a human white cane! 'Normal people would play netball,' the voice shouted in my head.

'I'd rather play, thanks.'

I heard Abby's sigh.

'OK.' And Mrs. Philips walked away without another word. She knew better than to try to change my mind.

I felt like running away to avoid the barrage of questions that I was inevitably about to face from Abby. How was I supposed to explain to her?

'Why do you ALWAYS have to say that!?'

'Dunno,' was the best I could ever be bothered to come up with.

'I know you'd rather do running with me than playing stupid netball!'

'Yeah.........'

'You get the offer every single time! Why did you.....?'

'Because..... I don't expect you to understand.'

And she certainly didn't.

We went out onto the field – Abby wasn't speaking to me properly – only responding with the occasional 'hmm' and 'yeah.' We did some warm-ups and Abby and I were practically dead by the time we'd run round the field a couple of times. Then we started the game and, of course, I didn't get the ball once. I spent most of the time standing still with my hands in the air like a scarecrow, just in case the ball should happen to fall into them. My class mates wouldn't dream of passing it to me on purpose. I don't think Abby did very well either. She gave me such a dirty look every time she had to run past me that even though I couldn't see her expression I could feel it. She must have been making it obvious on purpose. I suppose I would've been annoyed in the same situation.

By the end of the lesson I was feeling thoroughly fed up and miserable – and so was Abby, as she kept telling me. There was great frustration and humiliation in participating in a netball game, but that was not quite as bad as the humiliation of openly displaying my weakness on the field in view of all my classmates. They'd all come up and ask me why I was allowed to get out of games and some would call me 'lucky.'

Maths was last lesson. It was raining outside again, and the sky was dull, but it was still hot. When I came into the classroom I knew Miss Moore was back at the teacher's desk. She actually said 'hello' to me as I sat down. She wouldn't be so happy with me when she found out what I'd done – or hadn't done. She said the work wouldn't be too difficult today because we'd 'worked very hard in the last lesson.'

'I appreciate how much I left for you, but it's all important and we have to cover it at some stage.'

It turned out that the work had been algebra, which was one of the few topics that I found easier. Craig was, of course, one of the greatest protesters. He said that we should go to the government about it and that it was illegal to work at all in an oven. I giggled internally and drank in his creamy voice.

The work this lesson was just as difficult and boring as ever; Miss Moore had been lying. I often found that teachers did that. They'd just say that they were going to ease off to put you in a good mood for the lesson by trying to fool you into thinking that the work really was easier than usual. Maybe it was a tactic they learned at Teacher Training College.

At the end of the lesson I gave in my book. I must have looked as if I'd murdered someone as I put it on her desk because she asked me what was the matter.

'Nothing. It's just a bit hot.'

'I know. It wasn't like this over the summer.'

'It's impossible to work in this sort of heat.'

'You didn't find the algebra too hard did you, Louise?'

' No.' My feelings of stupidity increased so that I had to look at the floor and then almost run away from her. I knew it would be useless to try to explain myself – It'd all been my fault in the first place!

We all had to go to our form rooms at the end of school to find out about the work experience. I was desperate to get home so I'd be able to sit on my bed and have one of my episodes because once again I'd been really stupid and cowardly!

As I walked into the classroom there was the intermittent ripping sound of opening envelopes, followed by sighs of exasperation or relief. Everyone seemed just as nervous as I imagined we would be when we got our GCSE results. I took my envelope and ripped it open too. The paper inside was enlarged on my usual A3 sheet. At the top were all the expected things – name and address and so on. I looked down at the page .There it was in bold print:

'Firtops Residential Care Home for the Elderly.'

I read it a couple times before it sank in. I had been known in the past to misread things; one of my special talents, a very embarrassing experience when I read aloud: So I was going to be working with a load of old people? Cleaning their false teeth and spoon-feeding them?

I walked away to the bus in dismay.

***

Chapter 5

There was even more chattering than usual in the bus on the way home. All the people from my year were standing in a group at the back – a spot they'd adopted way back in year 7. They were rustling the envelopes and all the talk was about their contents. I could hear one boy moaning because he had been placed in a travel agent. His mates were laughing at him. I knew just how he felt.

I could picture it now; sitting in some tiny dingy room that smelt of pee, among hundreds of hunched reminiscing old figures, or maybe cleaning out a communal bathroom and toilets. If I was lucky I might even get to play a game of chess or cards in the 'day room.' In my mind this looked something like a village hall with hard plastic chairs and plastic cups full of weak, cooling tea and weak ageing men and women sipping it with toothless mouths.

Mum laughed when I told her, the way she always did at things I found extremely serious.

'You'll be a ray of sunshine for them. They'll ask you about all the latest fashions and pop music.'

Here was another thing I hadn't considered. I might have to endure painful hours of Cliff Richard and such like. I soon learnt the obvious. 'Care Home' meant that all the residents there needed care. In fact Firtops was especially for old people with disabilities. This made me feel even worse. I, of all people, should be even more tolerant than most shouldn't I? I read on my sheet that Firtops was a place where 'elderly people with disabilities were encouraged to live independent and fulfilling lives.' How could that be possible? I guessed it was some kind of guff to make them and their relatives feel better.

***

'Where've you been placed?' It was David. I'd known it wouldn't be long before he rang to find out. I'd left the form room before he'd arrived. I would have waited for him, but I'd had to catch the bus.

'Firtops Residential Care Home.' I put a fake enthusiasm into my voice.

'Oh.... That's nice.'

'No it isn't and you know it.'

He suddenly snorted with laughter...

'It's not funny.'

'Oh come on Louise, lighten up. It's not a touch on where I'm going.'

'Where's that then?' There couldn't be anywhere less attractive than my placement!

'An Opticians.' My views were changed instantly. Thank Goodness they hadn't put me there! Working all day with loads of people who were in the same boat as me and watching them being given back their sight.

'Oh,' I said. 'Then we'll be miserable together.'

'I'm not miserable.'

'What? You like the thought of watching people choose whether they want frames or contacts?'

'I don't care.' I knew by the sound of his voice he was smiling into the receiver. 'I have more important things on my mind than work experience. Anyway, it's not for ages.

He was right; it wasn't exactly an immediate problem. Not for a couple of months yet. There was something he wanted to say.

'Go on then, spill.'

'What?'

'You obviously want to tell me something.' He paused for a minute to add to the sense of drama.

'I asked Becky out.'

If I'd been drinking the glass of lemonade that sat on the table by the phone I would've spat it out all over the carpet. It was already obvious that she'd said yes. So now he had a girlfriend? With a start I remembered to be pleased, the way you should be when your best friend gets something he really wants, but I had to try hard to be happy for him. Was it because it wasn't fair; that I'd fancied Craig for much longer than he'd fancied

Becky? We'd whinged on to each other about how annoying it was. Now he'd made the step. I hadn't and probably never would.

'Remember the deal?' he continued. I should have known it couldn't be long before this was brought up. 'The deal' was that if one of us took the plunge, then the other would follow suit.

'That was only a joke,' I protested, sincerely hoping that he didn't honestly expect me to even think of asking Craig out. How could I? There was just no way!

'Come on, Louise. I was terrified when I asked her, but she said 'yes' and there's no reason why Craig won't.'

'Yes there is!'

'What?'

'He probably doesn't even know that I exist for a start.' Although the calculator incident had stuck in my mind there could be no way that it had remained in his!

'All the more reason for him to be intrigued.'

'All the more reason for him to think I'm some idiot who has a crush on him.'

David sighed.

'Isn't it worth giving it a go? What have you got to lose?'

'My pride...... My hopes of him ever agreeing..... I could go on.....'

He sighed again.

'Just think about it Lou. You might surprise yourself but it's obviously up to you.'

I knew he wasn't going to persist, and I knew that he'd drop the subject now unless I raised it. So if it had been up to him, things would have ended there. But now, for some reason my fantasies of asking Craig out seemed a more realistic possibility.

Next morning in the register there was a detention slip from Miss Moore, just as I'd expected. I knew what the green slip of paper that Mr. Campbell passed me was before I bothered to try and read it. I knew he must be annoyed with me. David seemed surprised. I'd been hoping I could put it away quickly before he noticed.

'What's that for?'

'Doing too little work in maths last week. It was impossible! Especially in that heat.'

'We should get days off when it's hot.'

'Hey look! Louise has got a detention! Take note everybody!' I got that sharp jolt in my stomach. It was Jamie Shawe. He was one of the privileged members of Craig's group.

All eyes must be on me now. A few of the kids were whistling in fake amazement. I knew that my image amongst my class mates wasn't good. I was too shy to ever speak to any of them and they knew that I worked fairly hard and actually did my homework. In the first year I'd been a much discussed subject among them. 'How come she gets sheets off the teacher? How come there's somebody in all her practical lessons? To do the work for her? Does she have learning difficulties?' Only the brave few had confronted me personally with these questions. Some had gone to David to try and get the 'inside story.' When I was asked I would struggle to try and explain and then blush and turn away. They must all know that I was ashamed of something, which probably made it a bigger deal for them than it should have been.

David had been with me since the beginning of first school. He was the only one I asked for help, simply because I knew him so well and knew that he understood.

I snatched up the slip and put it in my pocket. I didn't actually get to read it until break because David had persuaded me to go with him to meet Becky in the music block. They'd soon got into some deep conversation about different piano pieces. She was grade 4 and David had given up when he was twelve. However, he still managed to convince her that he knew what he was talking about, even though he'd never done a Grade at all.

I uncrumpled the green paper and saw it was written in that neat, large writing that Miss Moore used on her sheets for me in class.

'Louise. Please come to room 29 at lunch time for a half hour detention. This is for failing to do any of the work set in my absence.' I'd known she'd be angry.

I didn't really know Becky Myres. Besides History lessons I never saw her. And even then it was obviously David who spoke to her most. I soon began to feel that I didn't like her much. As I listened to her chattering to David (we had History next and I was very much ignored by them both) I decided that she was a bit like Abby. She seemed to agree with everything he said and she had a laugh that sounded really insincere. They were told to be quiet at least twice by Mr. Truman. I was gonna have to get used to this. Occasionally David would ask me what I thought about it to try to include me. I could tell he was aware that I felt left out.

It didn't take long for everybody to know about David and Becky. News travelled fast in our school. I wondered how everyone had managed to find out so quickly. I didn't think he was the type to publicise it. It must have been her. I imagined her gossiping with all her girlfriends about her 'new bloke.'

I shared the detention with Craig and some of his gang. There was that unmistakable voice as I came through the door. I should have known he'd be there. He was sitting on one of the desks, relaxed. He must be used to detentions.

'Louise,' called Miss Moore from the desk on seeing me. She already sounded angry and I felt myself turning pale. 'I want a word with you.'

The group at the back of the room immediately fell silent.

'What's she done, Miss?' It was Craig. Was I glad? He was actually acknowledging my existence again.

'Be quiet Craig.'

'What have you done, Louise? You naughty girl.' I'd forgotten that Miss Moore had just called me Louise and felt a rush of excitement that he knew my name. Too many emotions at the same time! Miss Moore took me into a corner and the group began to chat again. I was relieved. Explaining was going to be hard enough without them listening in as well.

'I'm really not happy Louise. When I went to mark your book there was no work at all. I checked the registers and you were here. This isn't like you. What were you doing all lesson?'

For some reason I hadn't planned an explanation. Perhaps it was because I was dreading it too much. But I'd have to think of one soon. I felt sick and flustered.

'It was really hot Miss. I didn't feel very well.'

'Everyone else managed to do satisfactory work in the heat.'

I hated the way all teachers did that. They were always talking about 'the rest of the class.' And I thought that schools were supposed to focus on 'the needs of the individual'. She was so close that I could hear her breathing. She was trying to make eye contact with me so I furiously looked away. Was I going to cry? She sat absolutely still and we must have stayed like that for hours.

'Well?' It was like a dog barking at me. I'd never realised that humans could bark like dogs, especially Miss Moore.

'I, erm..... it's just.....' I was stumbling over my words and I was dangerously near breaking point.

'I can't accept this kind of behaviour Louise. Perhaps she sensed how I was feeling because her voice was just a bit softer this time. 'You can't just decide not to work because it's hot. If I decided not to teach when I didn't feel like it, then no lessons would get taught, would they?' And that was supposed to be a bad thing?

'No. You erm...... Mr Ba....... the cover teacher....didn't give me your sheet...... I don't think you.... you told him about me.'

She seemed amazed.

'I've never heard an excuse like that before!' Her voice was hard and angry again, and maybe there was a bit of sarcastic amusement. Perhaps I shouldn't have tried to explain.

'You cannot use your disability to get out of work, Louise .Do you understand that?'

'Yes.' Now I really was going to cry. A tear slid down my face and I blinked. She must have seen it and she lay off.

'I don't want to see anything like this happen again. Go and sit over there.'

She pointed to a desk directly in front of the one Craig was sitting on. He was still chatting with his friends and was now looking at his watch. I tried harder than ever to stop any more tears. There was no way I could cry in front of him.

'Cheers Louise, you've wasted five minutes of the hell.' I smiled at him and he laughed!

Miss Moore was now handing out sheets of lined paper.

'You know the routine. 'I must complete all work in maths lessons or do the rest for homework.' Cover both sides please.'

'I didn't see the bit that said we had to finish it for homework Miss.'

'And I'm the Queen Mother, Craig.'

She sat down at her desk and was probably marking books now.

'You must all finish the work you haven't done as extra homework tonight.'

She came over to my desk and laid on it the sheets with the questions that Mr. Bald man had been using the other day. I stared down at them. This was what I'd been longing for so much. Just a stupid, boring piece of paper. And now I'd been told that I'd been 'using my disability as an excuse.' What an idiot!

I could hear Craig whispering to his friends behind me. Suddenly my stomach jolted and I strained to catch the words. His voice was thick, like Golden Syrup, even when it was in a whisper.

'You coming skating tonight?' I jumped again.

He was talking to Jamie Shawe. So he really was an enthusiast?

'Not if I have to do all this bloody work for tomorrow.'

'Bunk off then. Come on, there's this new move I wanna show you.'

'Can't we go on Saturday as usual?'

'There's loads of crap people on the rink on Saturdays. They'd get in the way.'

'Craig, seriously. I can't do tonight I've got stuff to do.'

'School stuff.'

'Ow!'

Craig must have hit him in the ribs or something.

'No..... Mel's coming over.'

'You're 'doing stuff' with her then?' They both laughed.

'I've asked Mel if she wants to come to the rink with me on Saturday. It's the only day she's free. She has to babysit her brothers and sisters on week nights. You coming

'Yeah, alright. I'll come.'

'Get there for the twelve o' clock session again yeah? That's when there's not so many people.'

'Whatever.'

I could hear them scribbling away at their papers as they spoke. Writing faster than I could think. I suppose they must have had a lot of practice.

'Louise.' I started violently. It was Craig that spoke. It was difficult to hear him over my heartbeat. I half turned around so that Miss Moore wouldn't notice that I wasn't writing. She must be used to all the chattering.

Craig was actually looking at ME, and me only. I basked in the moment. I was, at last, so close to him that I could actually see his face! He had large, dark brown eyes, just as I'd imagined.

'I saw you on the ice last Saturday for the first time with that David bloke.'

I felt mean afterwards, but I wished he hadn't seen David.

'He's really crap at skating.' Craig sounded as if he was trying not to laugh. He must be smiling at me. At me! I smiled back.

'I know.' I felt guilt digging at me.

'Are you going out with him or what?'

'No. Haven't you heard? He's going out with Rebecca Myres.'

Craig laughed out loud.

'Becky Myres?!'

'I know!'

Was that myself I could hear? That stupid put on voice? I had to speak quietly so as not to be heard by the teacher. How could I be so mean about David?

'Yeah, I remember seeing you now.' I said, as if I'd just noticed him on the rink out of the corner of my eye. As if he wasn't anything special.

'You're not bad at it. I haven't seen you there before.'

'No, it's the first time I've ever been.'

'The first time?! You must be a natural.'

'Be quiet you two. Get on with it.' I could have killed Miss Moore. How dare she ruin my moment!

He was now chatting to his mates again. I could just hear his words echoing through my mind. 'You must be a natural!' I wanted to ask him out there and then, but knew that would be stupid. I was the last to finish my lines. I handed in my paper way after everyone else had gone. Miss Moore must have wondered why I was suddenly so happy when I'd been about to cry a few minutes ago.

I almost danced out of the maths room, thinking about what Craig had said about going skating on Saturdays There was no way I could miss out on this opportunity. No way at all.

Chapter 6

Of course I had to go for a bit of skating practice for the next few weeks, just to check that success hadn't just been beginner's luck and to see if I was good enough to be worthy of being seen by Craig.

Sometimes I went with Abby or with another classmate, Naomi, as David was seeing Becky and trying to cram in homework every weekday evening. Once or twice I went alone. Naomi was one of those people who had the gift of saying funny things at just the right moment. She was popular and was friendly to everybody, which I envied in her. I wished I was a bit more like her. I didn't like going alone because you had to read off this screen to find out when each skating session began. And besides, it was boring on my own.

Abby was a terrible skater and I felt pride wash over me. If I was honest, one of the reasons I'd invited her was so that I could prove to myself that I was better than her at something. She was afraid of falling over in case she hurt herself. Naomi was average, but not as good as I seemed to be. I outshone both of them and they spent the whole evening saying how good I was. I kept denying it, but secretly rejoiced. This was the first time I'd had an evening like this for ages!

I didn't tell them that I'd come skating in preparation for impressing Craig one Saturday. It would have been far too dangerous. Nobody except David knew about my feelings for him. And if you told Naomi something in confidence it did have the tendency to be halfway around the school next day.

Abby didn't talk to Naomi much, although Naomi herself was gabbling non-stop to both of us. She didn't volunteer a comment and only spoke to Naomi when answering a question. She spoke to me a lot though, which at first I thought was rather rude. Thinking about it I realised that Abby wasn't the confident, daring person she appeared to be. At school she was always saying how she'd met various famous people and come out with witty remarks, but I could see how nervous she was of saying the wrong thing to Naomi. As for being daring; she spent the whole time clinging onto the side and I don't think she enjoyed it that much. I saw Abby in a new light that day, and my jealousy of her began to recede.

A week or two later David phoned me on Friday evening and asked me if I was free to do something the next day. Becky was going to come too. He thought it might be a good 'bonding process' for the two of us. I think he knew that I didn't like her much.

'Sorry, I've been neglecting you a bit lately haven't I? But you understand don't you? Becky's so nice.'

'Yeah.'

'And so good at music.'

'Mmm.'

'Imagine what you'd be like if you were going out with Craig,' he said indignantly. He did have a point. There would be nobody else left in the world if I was going out with Craig

'Anyway Becky and I want to see the new film that's out. What's it called?...... Addiction.' I knew that he wouldn't be interested in that kind of 'soppy stuff' normally. It must have been Becky's choice. Was she changing his personality? I groaned loudly.

'You really are playing by the rule book aren't you? What is it next? Dinner by candle light?' Why was I being so mean to him? I laughed to reassure him, and myself, that I was joking.

'What would you like to do then?'

I wasn't sure whether or not to ask him to come skating for a number of reasons. Firstly, I'd found out Craig's opinion of him and if he saw me with David it might not go as well as I'd hoped. And secondly, more importantly, I knew that David wasn't too keen on skating.

I eventually decided that it was safe to ask him. If he was with Becky then I could go off and talk to Craig if the magical opportunity presented itself. If necessary I could pretend that I had nothing to do with them. Of course I was being unkind but, at the time I couldn't stop myself.

'We could go skating.' He gave me the reaction I was expecting.

'Oh do we have to? I mean, I know you're all right at it but you've seen me skating Louise, I'm useless!'

'I happen to know that Craig's going to be there. Come on, it'll be a chance for me to do my half of the deal.'

I regretted saying that immediately, David might be expecting me to ask Craig out, and I had no intention of doing that. I would go up and speak to him at most, but the main aim of Saturday's visit I decided, would be to show that I could skate and to impress him.

David agreed reluctantly because I think he realised how much it meant to me. A spasm of guilt washed over me, as it occurred to me just how nice he was being and that, in a way, I was using him.

I planned everything whilst lying in bed that night. I'd wear my favourite blue jeans and that purple top I loved. I was hoping that David would ignore me, as he was always doing now when Becky was with us, so that I would be 'freed' from him. I didn't dare think about what it would be like if I actually ended up going out with Craig. Until now it had seemed that there couldn't possibly be anything bad about it; all the friends, the admiration – but if I was Craig's girlfriend I'd hardly ever get to speak to David again because of the way Craig felt about him.

I was glad that David knew the full story. He could point Craig out on the ice like he had done before. I couldn't think about that for too long. Craig was going to make everything bearable again, and I'd seen him properly now hadn't I? I'd recognise him myself. His words 'You're a naturall' played in my mind in that gorgeous voice.

I didn't usually wear much make up. I thought that people must look as if they were crying out for attention when they plastered it on. David said some of the girls in our class looked like they'd used cement mixers. And why did you need blood red kissable lips in school? Some were so bad that they had to be taken to the medical room to wash it off. I went for a slightly less subtle look than normal however. You don't need to guess why. I tied my hair up and made it stay where I wanted with vast amounts of hair spray. That was the only way with my hair. Even my Dad noticed that I looked better than normal which was quite something.

'Who are we trying to impress then?' I blushed and playfully hit him on the arm.

I met David and Becky outside the Leisure Centre. I could smell David's deodorant and I'm sure he had more gel on his spiky hair than usual. In my opinion Becky must be one of the 'cement' girls. Her hair looked far too pretty.

'Wow, you look lovely,' said David on seeing me. He looked at me for a moment and swiftly turned to Becky.

'You've been skating before haven't you?'

'A couple of times.... I'm OK.'

I sincerely hoped she wouldn't be better than me. Skating was my thing.

'Good luck with the Craig operation,' David whispered as we walked in. I grinned at him.

'I probably won't ask him; I just want to get to know him better.' My voice trailed off at the end of the sentence in a wobbly mess, making me realise how nervous I was. Becky had wanted to go to the one o' clock session of skating so that we could eat first. David and I convinced her to go with twelve and neither of us let on why. I think she sensed that we knew something she didn't.

It was fairly confidently that I took my first step out onto the ice. David nearly fell over as soon as he set foot on it and so did Becky, landing in his arms as if by accident. Luckily for me, a few moments later, Becky noticed one of her friends from school and was temporarily absorbed in conversation with her. It meant I could ask David the vital question.

'Is he here?' David's eyes swept the rink. I wanted to whisk them out and stick them in *my* head. I beat the frustration down. Now was not the time.

'He's over there with Jamie Shawe and a couple of other blokes.' I rejoiced. What would I have done if they'd decided not to bother?

'What's he wearing?' I was disconcerted as always, talking through gritted teeth.

'Just jeans and a T shirt.' I wanted to ask what colour T shirt? How many of them were in the group? What did his hair look like today? But, as usual, I couldn't.

'Good luck.'

I could tell that I was going to need it as I skated uncertainly, nearly falling over. I felt sick; not half as confident as I'd imagined I'd be. I must have skated round the crowd in the middle for ages, staring at all them all. Which one was he? He would be there, not round the edge with all the 'crap' people. Showing off to his mates perhaps. I searched all the groups of boys and I listened out for that voice. Here came that surge of frustration but I was going to ignore it. I needed to look good now. Why couldn't I just see him?! Anyone else would casually glance around and there he would be. I was beginning to feel my heart beating fast.

Surely it wasn't my name that I could hear someone calling? I must be feeling too hopeful and misheard. But this time it was unmistakable.

'Louise.'

I knew who that voice belonged to! The rich, low and wonderful voice that was always speaking to me in my head.

I managed to turn around; to my dismay almost falling over, and looked to see which direction it was coming from. Behind me stood a group of boys who were now all facing me. He must be one of them. I started to skate towards them. My legs were so shaky. It was amazing that I wasn't falling over. This was working! I was doing well for once! I knew I was smiling at the whole group, not concentrating on any of them in particular. Which one was he? Of course they were all wearing jeans and T shirts, apart from one who had adidas trousers and a baseball hat. I ruled him out. Then I noticed that one of them was a girl! I was caught in a flustered blur of mixed emotions.

Craig had actually remembered me from the detention! Well enough to bother to speak to me here on the ice! I was elated but at the same time extremely frustrated and worried. Why oh why couldn't I recognise him at this vital moment? I'd been suddenly thrown into a pit of confusion. I had been expecting to find him at my own pace; in my own time. Listen out for that voice and follow it. Wait for somebody to call him Craig or something. Wait till I was sure. But as it was I hadn't even planned what I was going to say to him.

I was drawing even closer now. It was nearly too late to decide what to do, what to say. I should come out with some comment to address them all, but what? The faces were growing nearer but still I couldn't tell which was his. I tried to see Craig's image in my mind, but it wouldn't come. Only the thought of his brown eyes. Why was spiky hair fashionable at the moment? I knew Craig had spikes, but so did all of them. Desperately I narrowed it down to two possibilities, but still I wasn't sure. They looked like twins. I must have looked stupid. I forgot that I was skating. Concentrating too hard on trying to decide what on earth I was going to do next......

I lay among them on the ice. My whole body was soaked and sore. My eyes were screwed up tight. I was aware of increasing pain from my arm. I wanted to scream but for some reason I couldn't. Perhaps it was because I knew that they were all around me. I could feel their eyes on me. I lay silent like that for ages. They must have thought I'd gone unconscious. I wasn't aware of what they were saying at first.

When at last I dared to open my eyes there was only one person staring down at me. Craig.

'Craig, I'm so sorry! I'm not as good as you at.......' I was frantically trying to speak through gritted teeth. I wanted to tell him that actually I thought I was going to die.

'Craig? Did you just call me Craig?'

That wasn't Craig's voice, it was Jamie Shawe's. It was obviously him now. His persona, the way he held himself.

Craig stood beside him. He'd gone to get help and some man with a red T shirt was crouching next to me.

'She just called me Craig,' said Jamie, gesturing with a horribly accusing arm at me. 'No, don't tell him!' I thought desperately. Everything was shattered.

'Are you... blind or something?' it was Craig's voice now, sounding a little bit anxious, although I didn't realise it at the time.

'No! I'm just stupid.' What I'd done was beginning to sink in. I screwed up my eyes again and tried not to breathe. I wondered if my arm was even attached to me anymore. Maybe it had been sliced off and had slid away to the other side of the ice.

'You are a bit aren't you?' It was Craig, laughing. Was this supposed to be funny? 'A bit of a David skater really. I wouldn't have called you over if I'd known you were going to kill us all. If you'd hit your head I'd say you were concussed!'

I felt terrible. I know now that they were only having what they would call 'a laugh' and I was probably expected to laugh too. But instead I cried. Tears poured down my face, I had no power left to control it. I didn't even feel the embarrassment which usually came when this happened in front of people. The pain was too intense. And them being nasty as well! It was too much. I wished that I could just lapse into unconsciousness. Then they, and this throbbing, might go away.

'Hey, we're only joking,' said Craig, seeing my tears. He sounded sorry and quite worried. But it was too late. I knew that I was going to have to teach myself to hate him. I couldn't even dream of ever going out with him now. Even if he was sorry. I

'Oh my God! Look at her arm!' Craig again. I'd made a feeble attempt to pull myself up off the ice, to get away from them, and in doing so, had exposed my left arm, which had been half hidden underneath me.

The attendant was putting something soft underneath it. I turned my head to look at it and then had to look away quickly. It was in a position which it could never bend to naturally, all sticking out at the elbow. Craig and the group were now huddled around a second attendant. The first was kneeling beside me and telling me that it was all right. I wanted to tell him that it wasn't anything near all right, and never would be again!

'It all happened so quickly.' One of the Craig gang was speaking to the second attendant. 'She was getting faster and faster as she came towards us and she wasn't slowing down to stop so we all had to suddenly move out of her way, except Darren who tried to catch her, but he got knocked over.'

It was then that I managed to scream. It wasn't loud and piercing like screams should be. It was small and pathetic with an agonised choke in it. I was getting past caring about Craig now. I couldn't bear this much longer. The group all looked down at me, speaking quickly, one after another

'Is she gonna be OK?'

'What's she done?' I realised that they were genuinely worried about me now. I screamed again so that I didn't hear Craig say,

'I was really mean to her. I didn't know she'd hurt herself.' Or at least I pretended to myself that I didn't hear it. I didn't want his pity.

'Louise! Are you OK? It's all right I know her.'

'What happened?' Becky was there too.

'I don't know.'

'Your arm!'

I managed to lift my head slightly and look around. The area had been shut off and all the skaters were confined to the other side of the rink. I was sure most of them were staring at me anyway.

***

I must have been in an ambulance. It was odd because I'd never been in one before and I'd always wondered what it was like. David was sitting beside me and Becky sat next to him. I wanted her to go away. I wanted David to focus all his attention on me and talk to me. Instead he was deep in conversation with her. It seemed like she was taking my place more and more.

'Look, she's awake.' David was staring at me.

'Are you OK?'

It was a stupid question really. The pain of my arm had gone for some reason but still I lay in an agonised state. Letting the tears roll down my face.

Chapter 7

'What's your name?'

'Louise Jordan.'

'How old are you?'

'15'

'What's the date today?'

'Saturday 27th of September.'

'Can you count backwards from ten for me please?'

'What?'

'Count down from ten.'

'Ten, nine, eight'.........'

A bright light was shining in my eyes. I tried to screw them shut against it. It was like at the hospital. But fingers were pulling them open and someone was staring into them. I wondered what on earth this was all for. A woman in a white coat was sitting on the end of my bed on wheels. Lots of people were milling about. I could hear children crying around me. I was in A&E.

David and Becky had gone somewhere and left me alone. My arm wasn't hurting. It was laid on the bed beside me, but I still couldn't look at it. It didn't feel like it was part of my body because of the angle it was at. It had gone all swollen but the pain had dulled. They must have given me something for it.

'.....Two, one.'

'Very good.'

'Who's the Prime Minister?'

'Tony Blair.' She was obviously satisfied with my little memory test.

'What did you want me to do that for?'

'We thought perhaps you'd hit your head on the ice and had concussion. You seem to be fine though. We're going to X ray it nevertheless, along with your arm.'

I wondered if this was because I'd called Jamie, Craig, but Mum later reassured me that it was a routine thing.

'You were out for a while you understand. But you must have just fainted.'

I couldn't recollect that, but I suppose I must have. Hadn't I wished for the pain to stop and the Craig gang to go away? I suppose it had come true. I was wheeled to another room where there were people lying on beds like mine. Maybe they'd broken some bone. For the first time it occurred to me that I might have. I'd never broken a bone before. I'd always wanted to when I was little. David had broken his ankle at primary school and he'd immediately become the centre of attention.

Mum came in through the swing door at the corner of the room, closely followed by David. Becky wasn't with him.

'What have you been up to then, Louise?' I was glad she was so calm about it. She'd trained as a nurse when she was younger so I suppose she was used to scenes like this. Now she taught English to foreign students, full time. I'd often wondered how it was possible to gain the enjoyment from it that she seemed to get. I didn't understand how language was formed, I just spoke it.

'Does it hurt? Have they given you some pain killers? I expect you've broken it.'

David looked really quite pale and shaken as he came to stand beside me.

'Thank God you're OK Lou. I was so worried! I was skating around with Becky – falling over of course.' He paused and I knew he was grinning at me.

'I was thinking about you. Hoping the Craig operation would go OK. Then suddenly loads of people were crowded round one corner of the ice. Apparently someone had fallen over and hurt themself. I made some joke to Becks about how easily it could have been me. I didn't think it could be you. But when I realised it was..... And you were just lying there with your eyes closed. You can imagine what it was like.'

I could, but didn't want to. Craig would also have seen me 'lying on the ice with my eyes closed' looking most likely like an utter idiot!

'I'm sorry,' he said suddenly, sounding more earnest than ever.

'Why?' I demanded.

'For not...... keeping an eye on you.' He soon realised that saying this was a mistake. I tried to sit up, furious. It was difficult because I could only use my right arm.

'I'm not a kid. I don't need looking after. This happened because I was stupid..... not looking where I was going.....not because of... anything else! You should know that.' I was doing my usual lying. I decided then and there that I never would admit the truth. Not to him. Not to anyone. Of course it had been because of my eyes. Everything always was. Normal people wouldn't have fallen over because they were concentrating so hard on trying to recognise somebody! David looked away, rather sheepishly.

'All right love?' said mum. 'They're going to take you down in a minute to look at your head and arm. What exactly happened? '

'I just tripped over somebody's foot.' This was going to be the story. Somebody with full sight could have done that easily.

'Oh dear! Dad had an accident once on the ice. I skated over his finger. Whose foot was it? Did they trip you up? Were they hurt too?'

'Mine, I'm OK.' David jumped in.

My head was fine and my arm wasn't broken.... my elbow was dislocated. Dad had often told me about the time he dislocated his shoulder playing rugby. The coach had put it back in when he was still lying on the field. Whenever Dad hurt himself he'd always say it was 'almost as painful as when he did in his shoulder.' I was terrified.

'Did it hurt when you did it?' Becky had joined us. She'd gone to ring her Mum to tell her where she was.

'Not too much.' I wanted to sound brave in front of her but I could tell that she'd seen through me easily.

'OK, it was agony.'

'How did you manage it? Me and David looked round and there you were. Why did you leave us anyway?'

'You know the way you fall over sometimes? People were skating a bit fast.'

There I was, lying again! I could hear Craig's voice in my mind. 'Are you blind or something?'

'A bit of a 'David skater' aren't you?'

'Hey! I didn't mean it.' I blocked it out. He must never know how much those words had hurt me. Or maybe he'd realised when I'd started to cry. In a way I was glad.

'We're going to have to give you an anaesthetic Louise.' It was another of those people in white coats. 'It's so that we can put your elbow back in place. Have you ever had one before?'

Only about a million times. When I was little they used to have to put me to sleep to check my eyes. It was the weirdest feeling ever. One minute you were waiting to fall asleep and the next you were awake again. You had no sense of time. Mum explained all this to them.

'When is the last time you had food?'

I remembered this too. Being denied breakfast on the morning of going to hospital. Wanting to go to the sweet shop in the waiting room.

'I had a Coke. I haven't had lunch yet.'

'That should be all right then.'

I was being wheeled away down one of those hospital corridors with the smell and the shiny floor. I watched the strip lights flying overhead like the white lines down the middle of a road as you drive along it. I could hear the clicking of the nurse's heels and the squeak of the wheels as we went along. So much had happened to me in such a short space of time and I hadn't had time to think. I was nervous. I began to cry. Only a little bit, so that the occasional tear would slip down my head and onto my ear.

'This might sting a bit.' A man was holding, what I assumed was a syringe with a needle in the end.

'I know.'

Memories of the old days. Wincing and then drifting into oblivion. I thought about how nice they were to you in hospitals. How they must get sick and tired of howling children and nervous patients. I was brave when they used to do this to me. I'd feel the needle go in and bite my little lips as I tried to listen to what they were telling me and think of something else. Just as I was doing now.

***

The first thing I noticed was that my arm was in a sling on my chest. Then I felt the pounding headache. I heard Mum's voice.

'Look, she's waking up.'

Three heads were peering down at me. Hers, David's and Becky's. I spent quite a while just drifting in and out of sleep, not really knowing what was going on around me. At one time I woke up and my arm was throbbing again, just like it had done on the ice. I could hear voices around me. A child was crying a couple of rooms down the corridor. 'No, no!' it yelled. Soothing voices were trying to calm it down.

Next time I woke up I could see the sun setting out of the window. I was in quite a large room with other beds in it, each with a curtain to isolate it. Mine was by this huge old fashioned window. It was one of those really lovely sunsets where the sky is all pink and orange and it looks like the world is on fire. The light shone into the room, illuminating the face of the person lying in the bed opposite. She had really long dark hair that was swept behind her head on the pillow. I imagined she must be asleep. I wondered what was wrong with her.

'Hello darling.' Mum had come up to see if I was awake. 'They're going to keep you in overnight because your hand is really swollen. You must have put it out onto the ice to save yourself. I don't think you've ever fainted before have you?' I shook my head.

'Where's David?'

'He and Becky went home. They've been here hours you know. Kept coming up to check on you. You're lucky to have such good friends.'

'I know.'

'Somebody might come up with some food in a minute if you're hungry.'

The girl opposite woke up and started to cry. She tossed and turned in the bed and then she was silent. I guessed she was in a drugged-up sleep; non-moving. Out in the corridor the noise of hustle and bustle seemed far away and mum just sat quietly. At last I had a chance to think about it all. To try to take it all in. Only this morning I'd had high hopes of speaking to Craig and getting to know him and becoming a good skater.

I allowed my mind to drift back over all the events. To relive the accident. Yet another replay! To my surprise I didn't feel too embarrassed. Instead I felt angry. Craig obviously hadn't known how serious it was when he'd started jeering. He couldn't have noticed my pain-stricken face or my misshapen elbow. Even so, how could he have said those things? And how come he thought he had the right to be rude to David? I recalled with shame how I'd gone along with him and abused David in the detention. Where was my loyalty?

Hadn't Craig said sorry, though, and then felt bad when he'd realised that I was seriously hurt? I felt the smile on my lips as I thought of his voice far above my head, playing like music. Then I made myself stop. How could I think about going out with him now? Did I even want to anymore? I thought I was unobservant! He hadn't seen how hurt I was, physically or emotionally. Craig was always teasing people. I was seeing him with new eyes. But you can't just turn off your emotions! I really felt that I could forgive all that if he came in right now and asked me to be his girlfriend.

All his mates knew about my accident too. I could hear them now. Talking about it in maths or in the playground; the hot news of the week. I'd never live this down. They'd all ask me at school 'how I did it', as if they hadn't heard already. They'd be asking me to see if I'd confirm the unbelievable story that was circulating the school. People who didn't even know me would see me and start whispering. 'That's the blind girl who bumped into Craig.' I was falling asleep again now. Craig had apologised. I'd never heard him apologise to anybody before. He must really care about me.........

60

Chapter 8

I had that sling on my arm for six weeks. It was OK at first, especially when I went back to school. Everyone seemed to be extra nice to me, moving out of the way and stuff and they kept asking what had happened. David and I had come up with a little story about how I'd tripped over his foot; how he'd been trying out some move and I'd got in the way. I was grateful to him for that and I hadn't even related the whole of the true story to him. I'd been trying to push it completely to the back of my mind and forget about the whole thing. I'd told him that Craig had been trying to impress his gang with one of his twirly things and he'd bumped into me.

The amazing thing was that nobody ever heard any different from Craig or his gang as I'd feared. I'd dreaded going back to school because of all the things they might have heard about me, but nobody came up to me and made a horrible joke about Craig and Jamie's likeness. Nobody made fun of my skating abilities. No one seemed to question my story. Craig and friends had either chosen to remain silent or had their good laugh before I'd been sent back to school. The latter was more likely. But imagine if Craig had been protecting my feelings…

I ignored Craig in maths. He never attempted to speak to me anyway did he? That was another relief. I'd been worried that he'd confront me and ask me what I'd been thinking of, or tease me, but everything went back to the way it had been before, when I was sure that he didn't know I existed. I convinced myself that this is how I wanted it. I didn't want him to be nice to me. I'd always think he was looking down on me and seeing the idiot in me all the time. Whenever I saw him I felt that shame. His voice still made me tingle whenever he spoke out and I fought hard from then on, not to be attracted to him. This was how it had to be.

Every time I thought about going out with him the way I used to I just recalled 'the incident'. I always called it that now. I couldn't bear to admit, even to myself, that I hadn't recognised Craig. I felt myself blush every time it came to mind. I couldn't even think of Craig without seeing that sea of blurred faces in front of me. How stupid I was! I let myself believe that David's story was true.

There was a letter one morning concerning my squint operation. They said I could come sometime in the summer to discuss it further and that most probably it would be fine. I was glad about that. I spent a long while studying my face critically in the mirror, which my nose almost touched. How much better I'd look if my eyes were completely straight! My left eye was slightly turned in, and grownups would ask mum why she hadn't taken me to the doctor about it when I was little and she'd had to explain. The op. would mean that that would no longer happen.

I was invited to Firtops one weekend to discuss what kind of thing I'd be doing there in the work experience week. Here was something else I'd been trying to forget. I was really nervous because I knew I'd feel shy of everyone there. I'd lost a lot of my self-confidence because of 'the incident,' I didn't even have the heart to skate any more.

My sling was still on. It wasn't fun anymore. I found mundane tasks a challenge. Everything had to be done with my right hand, which I found tired out really easily. I was fed up and wanted it to hurry up and get better. All the time it was in the sling I couldn't completely blank out the reason for it happening. I could feel myself getting more and more depressed.

Mum came with me to Firtops. In a way I felt that made me look a bit childish, but I knew I would've been even more nervous without her. I wore a nice skirt and top and brushed my hair into some sort of order. I hated my hair even more than usual at the moment. It was short and dark and too curly and it had a life of its own, going and staying where it pleased, which was usually in a large bush around my head. As for my eyes... They were so dark that you could hardly tell the coloured bit from the pupil. Apart from being slightly crossed they were too deep set. I seemed to be covered in spots today, despite all my efforts with various lotions, like I had chicken pox or something. It was just my luck when I wanted to look good. I'd spent about an hour with the mirror nearly pressed on my face. It wasn't as if a bunch of old people would care what I looked like anyway, but today all I could see was Abby with her lovely chestnut ringlets and piercing blue eyes, that everyone talked about. She had that lovely figure too, even though she ate more junk food than I did.

We set off at about 11 o' clock. Mum could tell I was nervous. I think she'd been a bit worried about me lately. I'd been constantly moody since the incident. Really rude to her and Dad and Mark. I'd spent quite a few evenings in bed in tears, replaying and replaying. Why couldn't I just see properly?! She'd tried to talk to me but, as usual, she was ignored. I think she knew that there was more to what had happened than I'd told her. It must have been strange for her to suddenly be shut out from me so much. When I was younger I used to tell her everything. Whenever something was wrong I would always go running to her, but these days I seemed to spend most of my life in my room alone. I wondered if she'd expected me to be like this about my eyes. Did she understand what I was going through? Mum was the only one who ever attempted the task of opening me up emotionally. My Dad was one of those introverted people who is a bit difficult to access. Rather like me.

Just the other week I'd thumped Mark. We'd been out shopping and he saw Craig across the street and whistled loudly at him. How dare he be able to recognise him! He'd cried and milked it for all it was worth and I'd got a huge row off Dad. 'What did you do that for?' he'd said, and I couldn't begin to explain. They must have thought I was crazy. I probably was.

It was one of those cool crisp mornings that you often get in October. Where the air isn't scented but it smells really fresh and cold. I didn't usually notice the changes in the seasons, but it was hard not to feel the chill wind that was bringing winter. There were loads of dead leaves everywhere. David and I used to go to the park together. There was a great conker tree where we used to collect bags full of them. We'd have leaf fights, chucking them all over each other.

There was a long drive which lead to Firtops. It had gravel along it and neatly trimmed hedges on each side. Behind them stood rows of tall fir trees which were silhouetted against the bright autumn sky. Mum described what I couldn't make out. She had always done that and still did. I never let myself believe that she was doing it especially for me. Apparently the drive split into two and in the middle was a circular lawn with a little brick fountain in the centre, encircled by a pool. There were a few flower beds around the lawn which were just full of earth. Already it wasn't like the Old People's home of my imagination.

The road joined up again in front of a huge white house with a black front door which had a ramp leading up to it. It was very impressive with four huge square windows on the bottom floor and smaller ones on all the rest. Perhaps it used to be a stately home or something. When I was young I used to love houses like that. I'd pretend I was a princess and it was my home. Beside the door was a placard which I imagined said 'Firtops.'

We drove round one corner of the house into a car park which was surrounded by extensive garden with ponds and what looked like a little summer house. Maybe the old people helped out with that. To one side of the car park were lots of little bungalow buildings. More modern than the house, mum said. Each had its own patch of garden. So this must be where they all lived? I tried to look at my face in the car mirror, pushed a stray strand of hair behind my ear and breathed in deeply.

'Louise? We've been expecting you. And you must be Mrs. Jordan. Please come this way.'

I was greeted by a woman with short blonde hair. The entrance hall had high ceilings and a varnished wooden floor on which my trainers made a loud squeak. To one side there was a very wide staircase with potted plants on either side of it. I wondered if they were real. In one corner was a lift and lots of big wooden doors around the room. It looked quite old fashioned but in a classy sort of way, not what I'd expected at all.

'My name's Mrs Symonds, I'm head of care and support.' Her voice was warm and friendly and it made me feel slightly less apprehensive. She held out a small hand. We were now walking into a room with a salmon pink carpet. It had armchairs arranged around coffee tables.

'This is the day room. If you'd just like to wait here I'll get Julia to show you around, then we can discuss what kind of thing you'd like to do here to help us out. We're looking forward to having you with us. We can always do with an extra pair of hands.' She touched my shoulder and I knew that she was smiling at me. There wasn't that smell of old age here either; of stewed tea, boiled sweets and wee. It smelt fresh and clean. There was none of that feeling that you might open one of the cupboards and find a dead body! I felt a bit silly for my previous feelings already. It was the kind of house where they might set a period drama.

Julia was a tall woman with dark blonde hair cut into a bob. She wore too much perfume.

'Hello Louise, I'm Julia. I'm a care worker here. That means I help the residents to get about and do things. We help them to do everyday things like washing and cooking as well. Just anything they need help with really.'

I was shown around the whole building – even the toilet and bath, which was raised at an angle with a little door on the side. I hoped that my services wouldn't be needed in this department! I imagined myself nervously standing next to a naked, wrinkly old woman and trying to lift her into the bath. I smiled to myself, then shuddered.

'So there's the main building where everyone can congregate in the day time. I thought I'd show you one of the flats so you can see what they're like. You'll probably spend some of your time helping individual residents.' I'd always been rubbish in a one-to-one situation. You had no choice but to be part of the conversation, and you had to constantly think of another thing to say.

'There's a very nice lady called Ellen who agreed to let us take a look. You'll probably see a lot of her. She's very friendly.'

We went through a little conservatory that was full of plants, a bit like a greenhouse but with garden furniture in it. Then we took a path beside one of the tiny lawns which had little plants all around the borders, splashed with colour. I could feel the nerves beginning to seriously kick in. I noticed a building nearby, which Julia told me was a swimming pool set a little way away amongst the bungalows. So these old dears went swimming?!

Ellen's flat consisted of a small living room with a three piece suite, a television and a chest of drawers. A bed was at the back of the room in the shadows and a kitchen and toilet were behind open doors to the side of it. Once again it was not the typical old people's flat that I'd imagined. More and more I was realising that it's actually impossible to make accurate assumptions about anything. This Ellen had obviously spent a lot of time making her room look pretty. Her chairs had pieces of material with flowers on them draped over the arms. But what caught my eye most was the fact that the white walls were covered with paintings and so was much of the floor for that matter. I wasn't close enough to see what they were all of, or how professional they were. There was one next to my head of a sunset over the sea. A calm, blue, sleepy sea like it sometimes looked at the harbour in the middle of the summer. I'd been there a couple of times and sat on the wall eating fish and chips. If I had a boyfriend that was where I'd take him. On a hot summer's evening it would be amazing, the sky ablaze with light. Once or twice I'd imagined taking Craig there, quickly put the thought away.

I brought myself back to the present. The painting captured the scene perfectly. I wondered who could have painted it. Perhaps Ellen was some kind of collector. There was another picture with a house set amongst a mass of greenery. It was huge and white with a brick fountain in the lawn outside it. Huge fir trees surrounded it and I realised with surprise that it was Firtops.

Ellen's flat didn't have that smell either. I was nervous about meeting her but I already knew that this wouldn't be a decrepit old lady. This person had character for sure.

A woman came into the living room from the toilet. She was small and in a wheelchair, and I immediately noticed and only just managed to stop myself from gasping when I saw that she only had one arm. As she drew even closer I could see that no legs protruded from her flowery skirt! I was horrified and tried to make a normal expression, as I realised that my mouth had almost jolted open.

'Ellen, this is Louise, Louise this is Ellen.' Julia stepped back as I stepped forward to shake the outstretched bony hand.

'Hello Louise, very pleased to meet you.'

'You too.' My voice was a croak. I'd been expecting her to speak with some sort of strange voice and I wasn't sure whether I should carry on talking. I looked down at her and she had a broad smile on her face.

She held a paint brush in her hand, and a glass jar of water in her lap. I realised with astonishment that she hadn't collected these pictures. She must have painted them herself! Why on earth was I feeling uneasy?! This was an experience that I was never going to forget. She pointed to a gold tin and told me to help myself to a sweet. I accepted gratefully and bent down to her chair.

'You only have one arm too.' She chuckled pointing to my sling. I remembered Craig calling me blind. But surely it was OK if she was saying it herself? How on earth could she actually joke about it! If it was me I'd be forever trying to hide away from the world, and mope about all day, and get all sensitive if anybody mentioned that I was different. I was already beginning to develop a deep admiration for this woman.

This was my first encounter with Ellen.

Around the middle of October I had one of those days when everything seems to go wrong.

First of all, I was half an hour late for school, which was all Mark's fault. Today was the day when he was due to have his BCG injection; something that everyone had to have in year 9. Mark had an irrational fear of needles, inherited from my Dad, I think. I remembered my BCG and how much it didn't hurt; so I kept telling him. But he wouldn't have it. He spent the whole morning whinging to mum about how he wasn't going into school. When Mum finally gave in and said he could have the day off, he whinged even more because he was scared that if he didn't have the injection he'd get TB because he wouldn't be immune to it.

He was being extra annoying this morning! He was acting like he used to when he was about six. Afterwards, when I'd taken the time to bother to put myself in his shoes, I felt sorry for him. It must be horrible to be that scared – he was nearly in tears. It was quarter to nine and he was still refusing to get in the car, but he wouldn't let us drive off either.

'For Goodness sake Mark!' I shouted. 'It's just an injection. It doesn't even hurt.'

'Oh shut up! This has nothing to do with you.'

'Yes it has. You're making me late and I'm gonna get in trouble again!' Oh great! I bet now he was going to go on about why I said 'again.'

'Look, be quiet the pair of you!' It was Mum. She'd managed to stay calm and sympathetic to Mark until now. 'Mark. For goodness sake come or don't come. I'm going now, with or without you. What's it to be?'

Mark slouched down in the car, not looking at me. He really was trying not to cry. Just then however I was too busy looking at my watch to have any sympathy.

I got a late detention. Even nice Mr. Campbell couldn't save me from that. By the time I got to school first lesson had started. PE was a good lesson at the moment because of my arm. Abby was in a really bad mood all lesson because it meant that she had to participate in the game and look 'a right prat.' How was I supposed to sympathise with her?! I couldn't help it if I'd dislocated my elbow, could I?

After PE Abby announced that she was getting 'weekly' singing lessons. I only just managed to avoid biting her head off. I'd been nagging Mum for them for nearly a year, but they were 'so expensive these days and I had a lovely voice anyway.' Now Abby would probably get really good and leave me sounding like a frog in comparison. I stomped off to History.

History was another nightmare. It hadn't been fun for a while anyway because David would spend the whole lesson quietly chatting to Becky and ignoring me. Mr Truman had decided to use a different text book today because it covered the Cuban missile crisis in more detail.

The print was tiny.

'David this is way too small,' I whispered reluctantly. I had to whisper so that Mr Truman didn't hear.

'Tell him then.' And David gestured to the teacher. I was completely taken aback. He'd usually just agree to write it down for me.

'Couldn't you just write the questions bigger in the back of my book?' I was blushing. I sounded like a spoilt child. He was obviously annoyed. I must have interrupted an important conversation between him and Becky.

'For God's sake Lou. Just ask him!'

'No...'

'All right then. If you won't I will.' He put his hand up and I gave him the dirtiest look I could manage.

'David. Don't.' This was the side to him I had only ever glimpsed before. He wasn't making any effort to be nice about it

'Why not?'

Perhaps this was a question that he'd wanted to ask me for ages, but only now found the courage because of Becky. I felt like I was going to cry and hit my breaking point, right here and now. I couldn't answer him.

'Yes David?' Mr. Truman must be looking over at us.

'Could you enlarge these pages for Louise please?' he said holding up the text book.

I wanted to hide my face in my hands.

'Oh yes. Sorry Louise. Do you always get other people to ask questions for you?' The whole class laughed at his horrible joke but I was on the verge of breaking down. I blinked fast and gulped and gripped my plastic chair with my fists. Mr Truman walked out of the classroom to the photocopier in the library telling us to 'start the work.'

'Well thanks a lot!' I couldn't believe David had done that. This was much worse than if I'd asked myself. Now everybody knew that I couldn't cope.

'What? You weren't going to ask. So what was wrong with me doing it? Someone had to.'

Again I couldn't answer him and I kept gulping to try and avoid those pathetic tears.

He paused, wondering whether or not he was brave enough to say anything else.

'Grow up, Louise.' I could tell that he didn't mean to say that with such harshness, but then he turned away to Becky and started talking to her again.

I spent break time sulking in the toilets and trying to cry inaudibly. The girls outside were talking about who fancied whom, and applying the cement to their faces. Using the toilet was a trial with my arm. I was sick of it.

I didn't see David all day except in our lessons but he might as well have not been there because we ignored each other. I was too angry with him and he probably was with me.

When I got home Mark was whining about how his BCG was hurting.

'Shut up Mark! Go to your room and have a good old whinge if you really have to.' I had already been to mine and had passed my breaking point, almost howling down the stairs like the big baby that I was. Why had I not done years ago what David had done today? We were such good friends! What if it was all over now? Surely I hadn't just been thinking of him as my 'carer'? To round the day off Dad was in a mega-mood as well. I suppose it's infectious. He insisted on watching the news when *the Simpsons* was on the other side. Usually he let us watch it and waited for the ten o 'clock bulletin. But he and mum were going out tonight and besides he 'shouldn't have to answer to me because it was his TV and he paid the license'. Why couldn't I have my own TV anyway? I'd be able to put my stupid nose nearly against the screen and see everything properly. I'd been crying so much that I had an awful headache and couldn't imagine what the future was going to be like now that David wasn't looking out for me. That's how it was wasn't it? I was such a big, idiotic baby!

I slumped down in my usual chair in front of the TV and kept sniffing and trying not to pinch my arm. I would have gone back upstairs to sulk in my room, (there should be a cot in there! I was such a big baby!) but I couldn't be bothered. Instead I raided the biscuit tin, as usual, and sat in front of the TV as the news started. I yawned and pinched my arm just one more time. What was I gonna do? It was all my fault! I'd known this for years and now it had only been verbally expressed by my best friend! I scowled at the screen in front of me so that Mark couldn't see my tearful face and ask me for the hundredth time 'why the hell I was crying when *he'd* been the worried one this morning.' Abby had a TV in her room with VCR! And she was getting singing lessons! Everything was going wrong and nothing was working in my favour. I was sick of my sling and I wanted to have my arm back again.

David didn't know how often I cried on my bed and how difficult everything was all the time for me did he? Why did he have to tell me to 'grow up' anyway? It was all so unfair that he could see whatever he wanted! He could just pick up anything and read it and never go through the humiliation and embarrassment of having to admit that he couldn't. He'd changed so much after meeting Becky. Before, he used to try to understand and sympathise about my eyes but now he didn't care! What had she been saying to him? That I was a pathetic idiot? Well, even if she had, it was true wasn't it?

Mark started on about his arm again. At least both his arms were working at the moment! Dad told him to shut up.

Why couldn't I afford singing lessons like Abby? For all anyone knew my lack of money could be stifling some hidden talent. I felt like the unluckiest, stupidest person in the world.

Dad had turned up the TV in response to Mark's whinging. Mark flounced out. The news reader was talking about yet another famine in some war-torn country. I was about to retreat into self-pity again and wallow when the pictures came on. Thousands of black faces were peering at me through the screen. Thin, black sticks, with huge empty eyes. Somebody was handing out sacks of grain and they were looking at is as if it were chocolate cake. It looked dry and disgusting. I wished that I was sitting on the sofa instead of my chair by the TV; then I wouldn't be able to see them. I picked up the last of three chocolate digestives and was about to shove it in my mouth but I found I couldn't. I tried to switch off again and think about something else. Like what? Like all the things that had gone wrong for poor me today?

Because Mum and Dad were going out tonight, Mum was getting fish and chips. Dad turned off the TV and tutted. I pretended that the only reason I was relieved was because it was the 'boring news.' The lovely smell filled the air as she walked in

I was starving.

Chapter 9

'I'm sorry Lou. What I said before...... It was out of order. I hope it won't make any difference to you and me.'

I wanted to tell David that he'd really hurt me but I couldn't stay angry at him for long.

'It's OK,' I said in a dull voice. I sensed that he wanted to say something else about it but thought better of it. We started talking about this rubbish single we'd heard on the radio that morning and how songs like that shouldn't be allowed. I was laughing again, but an uneasiness lay between us.

The month or so that passed before I actually started work experience at Firtops went by without me really noticing it. I hadn't spoken a word to Craig and obviously he hadn't attempted to say anything to me either. He didn't even mention the fact that my brother had whistled at him in the street.

Nothing out of the ordinary happened. I was asked to read from a text book with tiny print and I made an utter fool of myself and ended up on my bed in tears as usual. Why was this still happening? Why had I still not managed to do anything about it? But nothing major happened like 'the incident.'

David was still going out with Becky. I was seeing less and less of him these days. We used to spend most Saturdays together and sometimes the evenings after school. But now he was 'doing something with Becks.' He was very fond of her I know and, because I was supposed to be his friend, I let it go by. Besides, I wasn't feeling particularly sociable towards him.

I was anxious about work experience and my eyes were, probably literally, driving me mad. Ever since the incident more and more seemed to be happening to make me think about them and more and more I couldn't help thinking that somehow I had to change.

I didn't sleep on the Sunday night before I had to go to Firtops. I lay awake for hours considering everything that could go wrong. I probably wouldn't recognise anybody, and maybe I'd get lost. Ever since I'd had that brief meeting with her I kept thinking of Ellen as well. I could recall clearly all the feelings I'd had on first seeing her and I felt ashamed. I could still feel the horror rising in my stomach as I saw her incomplete body. The idea I'd had that her voice would sound funny. The inability to know what to say. OK, I was really shy anyway, but I'd felt as if it would be like talking to an alien.

I had a strange fascination with Ellen. It had certainly been a shock to my system to find someone like her, a wonderful artist, in a place where old women with no interests other than bingo were meant to live. The main reason that I couldn't leave the thoughts alone was because it was the first time that I had any idea how other people sometimes saw me. Before I'd thought they were just ignorant and stupid. The number of people who asked me if I needed glasses! As if I wouldn't wear them if they helped!

Mum drove me to Firtops on her way to work. I was too nervous to be suffering from my lack of sleep. I wondered desperately if they knew about me. I met Mrs Symonds at reception again in the lovely entrance hall. I'd forgotten how huge it was. We'd had a discussion after my meeting with Ellen about what they were actually going to do with me. I can't deny that I felt a bit out of place; wondering if they saw me as a burden rather than an 'extra pair of hands'. I'd said that I'd 'like to help out' which sounded silly now. What else was there to do?

We'd come to a decision that my services would be placed wherever they were needed. Apparently Ellen found it useful to have somebody with her to help her with the paints.

'She can manage on her own.' Mrs Symonds had said,' but she finds it speeds things up a bit. She gets money for those paintings you know.'

I wondered if this was the only thing they could think of for me to do. It was very kind of Ellen to let me intrude on her if this was the case. She was the first person I was sent to that morning. Maybe they'd put me with her first because we'd already met and they wanted to be kind. Mrs Symonds said Ellen was in the middle of painting a 'masterpiece', using lots of different colours.

On entering the flat I saw her straight away, sitting in her little green chair with the paint jar in her lap. I jumped in spite of myself and then pinched my arm hard.

'Good morning, Louise.' Her voice surprised me again and I blushed in spite of myself.

'Hello Ellen.' I hoped it wasn't obvious how nervous I was.

I looked down at the big canvas that lay on an easel next to her, set very low. The bottom was covered with a green wash.

'Well I'll leave you two alone then,' said Mrs Symonds. I felt a slight tingling sensation up my arms and I shuddered. It almost felt like a prison sentence. I was going to have to try and make conversation with Ellen now.

'We'll call you if we need you anywhere else.'

'OK.' It was that stupid little mouse voice that spoke again. Ellen must think I was one of those schoolgirls who just sat and watched you and only ever came out with single word answers. I wished I could tell her that I wasn't. I wanted to tell her that I admired her paintings and her talent. Instead we sat in a long silence with only the swishing of her paintbrush to break it.

'Your arm's mended then.'

'Yeah.' I was surprised she remembered and also felt a bit guilty. Maybe to her this was like people getting glasses was for me.

I looked around the little room. The carpet was grey with a few coloured patches where paint had been spilt. On the chest of drawers there were lots of, what looked like, photographs in little frames. I wondered what they were of. Out of the window it had started raining heavily, making the patio all shiny, and big brown muddy puddles were forming in the flower beds. How did she manage to paint such a sunny picture when it was like that outside?

'Which school do you go to?'

'Haslecombe.' It was still that stupid little squeak.

'What subjects do you do there?'

'The usual. Maths, science, history, English.' It was boring small talk. I wanted to ask her how she got into art in the first place. About her life. Had she married? It crossed my mind that maybe she was a bit shy too. I felt uncomfortable. She didn't need me here. I expected she liked the peace of being alone to paint.

'It's very kind of you to let me sit with you.' I'm not usually one to put forward a sentence of my own accord. I felt as if I'd been here for hours.

'It's very kind of you to come and help me.' I think she was smiling at me, so I smiled back. The ice was beginning to melt.

'You don't need me.' I said laughing.

'Oh I know I don't need you. But it's lovely to have a bit of company sometimes. You don't know how lonely it gets here on my own, just me and my paints, and Talk-Show hosts aren't much company.' She gestured to the TV which was switched off. I could see I'd unlocked her now. She seemed to be the sort of person who is a bit awkward at first but, once the initial formalities are done with, reveals her true colours. This was useful as I was inclined to follow her lead and forget my shyness. She asked me for a drink of water

'That speeds things up a bit; very naughty of me.' She said, laughing. She drank the water, using it to swallow some pills. So they were in charge of their own medication here?

She must have seen me looking at her curiously.

'It's a wonderful place to live,' she said. 'We are in charge of our lives, they are here to offer support.' She seemed like such a happy person!

'What kind of music are young people into these days?' she continued.

I smiled. 'Anything really, as long as it has a rhythm. Most pop singers can't sing in my opinion.'

She chuckled. It sounded like running water.

'I'm more into classical myself.' There was another short silence.

'Do you sing?' I looked up from staring at the floor and laughed nervously.

'I'd like to.'

'I used to sing once in a choir at church. I could sing you any hymn. I don't sing any more though. The others don't really appreciate my talents in that field.' She laughed again and I laughed too. 'I stick to painting nowadays. Do you fancy a cup of tea?'

'Yeah. Shall I make us a cup?'

I wandered off into the little kitchen, glad to be given something to do. Everything in it was miniature. A tiny fridge in one corner next to a sink and a doll's house cooker. It was also very low down so that I had to bend to get to the fridge.

There was a kettle on the sink and I found some tea bags in the cupboard and milk in the fridge.

'What do you like doing?' I heard her call from the living room.

'Lots really,' I called back over the bubbling water. 'As well as singing, I like listening to decent music, reading.' If very slowly.

'Do you play an instrument?'

'No.' I'd always wanted to play the flute but you had to sit miles away from the stand and I'd never be able to read the sheet music. Of course I didn't tell her that. I'd forgotten about my eyes until now. Did she know? I made myself stop thinking along those lines.

I brought the steaming tea into the living room in little china cups with roses on. I wondered if they were hers or if they belonged to Firtops. I wanted to know about her past. Were those photos of family?

'Can you hold a harmony when you sing?' she asked. I could a tiny bit, but I sincerely hoped that she wasn't going to try and get me to sing something now. Was she an amazing singer as well as brilliant painter?

'Yes, sort of.' I laughed properly at the thought of us singing together without trying to learn anything first.

'I can't!' she said. 'I tried quite a few times for fun, but nobody wanted to sing with me.'

I thought of me trying to get David to sing in harmony with me. I'd asked him once because I was too shy to ask Abby. I laughed at the thought of David and me trying to harmonise.

'It takes me a long time to learn a harmony properly,' I said.

We carried on chatting about this and that and I really felt that I was getting to like her. I was almost totally at ease; not finding it so difficult to think of things to say.

'I want to finish this clump of daffodils in the corner,' she said, gesturing towards her huge painting.

'Could you pass me those two yellows there?' There was a box by my feet full of tubes with coloured lids. She must mean that they were in there.

I picked up the two tubes of yellow that were on the top of the pile and gave them to her. I heard the sound of her squeezing paint onto her pallet, but giving a grunt of annoyance as she squeezed the other tube.

'I've forgotten when I last used that cadmium yellow,' she said. 'It's completely dried out. Could you get me another from the top drawer over there?'

I walked over to the chest of drawers, where I was able to take a closer look at all the photographs that stood on top of it. They were all of people who appeared to be residents here. She must be a sociable lady, a pillar of the Firtops community perhaps?

I opened the polished wooden drawer and a musty smell greeted my nostrils like in a museum. The drawer was lined with crimson velvet and dust flew up at me as I pulled it open. I coughed.

'I haven't had to use paints from that drawer in a while,' said Ellen. 'It's mainly been only the ones in this box lately.'

The drawer was full of tubes with different coloured lids. It looked like something out of an art shop. There were blues, greens and reds and three shades of yellow in the middle of the bottom row.

At first I wasn't worried by this, I picked up each in turn, searching for the word 'cadmium' on the side. To my untrained eye, each shade on the lids appeared the same, or very similar. Of course the writing on the tubes meant nothing to me. And then I realised what was happening, as my reasonably successful day turned into yet another nightmare.

'Which one was it you wanted?' I said weakly. What was I going to do? Again I knew what I should do. Ellen wouldn't mind. She of all people wouldn't mind. So she didn't know? I would just tell her. But, once again, the words wouldn't come.

'Cadmium,' was the easy response from behind me.

I rummaged hopelessly around in the drawer to pretend that I was looking for it for what seemed like forever, hoping that some magic way out of this would come in a minute. Maybe a fire alarm would go off and I'd be free.

'Isn't it there?' I looked at Ellen. Her head was still bowed over her work. She couldn't know what was happening.

'No....I.....er...' I heard her move in her chair and I could tell that she was now looking at me. My desperate voice had attracted her attention. I was hopelessly holding the three tubes of paint in one hand and standing staring at the wall. I was useless! Then the rational side of me managed to feebly present itself. I swallowed hard and cleared my throat.

'I...erm...well....I......'

'I can't find the paint you want because I don't see well enough to read the labels?' Ellen's voice cut me off and I started violently, wondering if I'd managed to explain without noticing. She'd spoken in a very matter of fact way. She'd said what I'd wanted to say. How did she know? I was helplessly confused.

'That's all you have to say, it's as simple as that.'

I didn't want to look round at her. I felt the tears rising. I didn't have the power to stop them as I usually did. I'd been caught off guard, like at the ice rink.

'Mmm'. My voice was higher and squeakier than it had been all day. I sniffed like that baby part of me and reluctantly turned to face her. I didn't know what expression was on her face, so I imagined it. Perhaps she was disgusted at me for being ashamed of being disabled. She'd have good reason after all.

'Come here,' she almost whispered. I moved mechanically without bothering to stop and consider why.

'Have a seat.' She carefully put down her paintbrush and then patted the chair next to hers. I was so close to her that I had to try as hard as possible to stop the sniffing and breathe normally. Now I could see her face. It was full of not pity but empathy. It was full of understanding and just from this look I could tell she knew how I felt. For once in my life somebody really knew and understood how I felt.

The look only lingered for a few seconds. It was as if she was reliving her past or something.

'I'm sorry Louise.' She said quietly. 'I was told about you by Julia, and I must admit I completely forgot. That wasn't very sensitive of me was it?'

I couldn't find the words to answer.

'I mean, it's like somebody asking me to walk isn't it?' she smiled and I tried to smile back. I was amazed by her. Once again she was able to joke about it.

'Tell me to be quiet if you wish Louise. It's none of my business I know. But your disability is obviously something you're finding a real trial. I know how that feels. I really do. But, there is a way to cope with it. Have you ever thought about why it's so difficult for you to admit you can't see? Things could be a lot easier for you if only you could, you know.'

I could have said 'yes but I'm so stupid that I can't come to a conclusion.' Instead I shook my head.

'Think about it Louise, it's incredibly difficult to deal with I know. But you can make it onto the road to recovery. I used to hate it when people reminded me that I was different. But everyone has their differences anyway and once you accept it. My goodness me, life is so much easier!'

I was sure that what she was saying was true, but I didn't want to think about it. I wanted to pretend. She was forcing me to face it, and I hated it. I could feel her hand on my arm. Not giving patronising pat, but she actually knew how I felt. The door opened at that moment and Julia came in. She seemed slightly startled but I hastily stood up and pulled my hair back behind my ears.

'Will you come and help to serve the dinners in the Day Centre?' she asked. 'One of the staff is off sick and we could really do with a hand.' I agreed willingly. I was very relieved to get away from Ellen, because she had made it so that to face her was to face my problem, and, besides, here was a chance to really be useful.

'Think about it Louise,' she kept saying in my mind.

Chapter 10

The dinners at Firtops looked really nice. Not the mashed up, completely unidentifiable goo that I'd expected. Nice salad rolls and soups and burgers and chips. I was really hungry by the time I'd finished. All the time I was helping I could smell it.

I laid the tables. There were about ten of them around the room. Each place needed a mat made of some funny woven straw, a knife and fork and a napkin folded up into a glass. Julia showed me how to do it so that it made a little cone shape that stuck out of the top. Each table had a large vase in the centre with blue silk flowers. I built up a kind of rhythm. Placing each knife and fork down to a certain beat. I made myself concentrate on doing this to avoid the main issue in my mind. I was frantically trying to ignore what Ellen had advised. I didn't want to 'think about it.'

When everybody came in I was a bit daunted. They were all chatting and laughing with each other. Some, however, were extra friendly and went out of their way to talk to me. A couple of women came up and asked how I was getting along. As I watched them taking their seats I couldn't help picturing myself among them in years to come. Sitting at the end table alone sipping tea with a toothless mouth. I was terrified of the thought that I might still have the same feelings about my eyes when I was old. I might still be living in my fantasy and I would have missed out on all the good things I could have achieved in life because I hadn't had the guts to ask for help.

I listened to their conversations. A crackly voice screeched into a hearing aid. 'Would you like beetroot, Alf?' One lady had a black dog sitting next to her. I didn't think you were allowed pets in care homes. I was told that residents were able to cook and eat in their own rooms, but most of them had obviously decided to come here. Was it because they were sociable?

I settled for a bowl of chips and a salad. I felt uncomfortable; not knowing where to sit or whether places were saved for friends. It would have felt strange sitting among the residents anyway. I might have to join in the conversation that was going on at the table I was standing next to. Or worse still I'd sit in silence and they'd all gossip about me when I'd gone. I suddenly spotted the pretty green dress that Ellen had been wearing. She was sitting among them at the table beside me. Green suited her. I felt her presence at the table was all the more reason to find somewhere else. I found myself dithering in the middle of the hall with my tray until a lady brushed past me and knocked my lemonade all over me. She was a bit too sorry I think. I was sure she must 'know' about me because she kept touching my arm and asking if I was all right. She offered me a seat next to her at a table full of perms and I politely refused. There was one in the far corner that looked empty and I almost ran to it. I was quite content to eat alone now. Everyone had probably noticed me just standing there in the middle of the room.

As I looked up I noticed a boy sitting across from me, but by the time I'd seen him it was too late to turn and find somewhere else. This could be even worse than sitting at any of the other tables. At least then I could fade into the background. Was he one of the staff? None of the others seemed to be here. He was probably asking himself the same about me. He had dark brown hair that curled over his head. I felt awkward as usual when faced with someone new. I knew I should introduce myself but I couldn't think of what to say. That was always happening to me .If a conversation was started we'd have to keep it up all lunch or else sit in embarrassed silence.

'Your name's Louise isn't it?' he said. He sounded really young.

'How do you know?'

'I recognise you from school. I've seen you around sometimes with that David bloke. I'm Nick.' He didn't seem shy and I was glad. He'd be able to do most of the talking and I could just mm and er a bit.

I'd never noticed him around before but then I suppose I wouldn't. All of my recognition came from voices and the way people said things or what they were wearing or their hairstyles.

'I wasn't expecting to be placed somewhere like this,' he said. 'It's not the kind of thing you expect a boy to do is it?'

The staff I'd met so far were all women. I suppose Firtops in general was quite a feminine environment.

'I only wrote that I liked working with people on my form. I thought I'd end up somewhere like a dentists. Surprisingly enough this is more interesting. It took me yonks to fill in that form. I didn't really know what to write. If I'd put that I was into woodwork they might've put me in a shop. I hate shop work. My Saturday morning down the supermarket's bad enough.'

I wanted a job. I hardly ever had any money except when Mum and Dad were feeling generous. But I wasn't bold enough. The numbers on a cash register would probably be small and even a paper round involved roads and cycling and reading house numbers. Lots of my friends seemed to have shopping sprees every week end.

'How are you finding it here?' he asked and I realised from here on that I was right. Shyness was not one of his shortcomings.

'Fine,' I said. I desperately wanted to expand on this to expose my personality and not my front.

'I've mostly been with somebody called Ellen, she's very nice.'

'Which one's Ellen?' Nick looked around the noisy room. I pretended to look for her, hoping to find the green dress that didn't seem to be anywhere.

'I don't think she's here.' My voice had acquired that little weak quiver which it always got in these situations. I knew she was in here, I'd seen her come in. 'Think about it Louise, why can't you admit it?' I pushed her words furiously away.

'I've been helping in the garden,' he told me. 'There's not much to do at this time of year, but they like to be out there anyway. I can't think of anything more boring than gardening. I feel like a right Alan Titchmarsh!'

Fortunately my services at Firtops were needed elsewhere after lunch. I was glad that I actually had been asked to give assistance at lunch time, which had taken my mind off Ellen. I was in the laundry room ironing all afternoon. It was boring. People just drifted in and out – mostly women – and picked up their clothes. A couple of ladies, called Mary and Edith, were with me all afternoon. Their only topic of conversation seemed to be the lives of their fellow residents.

'You'll never guess what happened to June.'

'June? No what?'

'Half her washing blew over the fence into the field and we had to get the farmer to give it back.' Edith had a West Country accent.

I went to the harbour at Haslecombe after I'd finished. Firtops was only a few minutes' walk away and there weren't any roads without traffic lights, probably to aid the old people. I'd been wondering all day what to do while I was waiting for Mum to finish work and collect me. I could have gone home straight away if I'd caught the bus. But I'd have had to swallow my pride and accept help in doing it. It would be like holding out a white cane.

The town of Haslecombe is quite big, but you have to go further afield for sight-seeing. Even though it's right on the sea it's not that touristy. It's very pretty though. Lots of really old houses and cobbled streets. That's another reason why I liked it. Pedestrians were the only danger; no cars except on the surrounding roads.

The harbour is lovely too. It's only a little one, which was just in front of me, beyond a low dry-stone wall. There are a couple of chip shops along the sea front which gave it that smell. And there were loads of sea gulls about, to keep in with the atmosphere. I wished I lived in Haslecombe. Then I wouldn't have to nag Mum for a lift every time I wanted to go into town. I really wanted to be independent, but I'd have to make all that effort to achieve it. I couldn't admit that I would have to take more steps than most to do the same things that they did. Those thoughts were crowding into my head again now. Why couldn't I admit to it? I didn't want to but I knew that soon I'd have to 'think about it' as Ellen had advised.

I could feel the sea breeze on my face, nice and refreshing, and the salty taste on my lips. I always liked to sit on that wall and listen to the waves and the boats chugging in and out. Sometimes in the summer I'd go swimming at the beach a few miles away on the other side of the town. It was freezing in the water, even on scorching hot days. Hardly anybody would ever brave the cold with me and I'd often be out there on my own in the holidays. But usually I'd just sit here and hear and feel and smell the wonderful atmosphere. Like some of the people at Firtops who sat in their chairs and gazed out of the window.

The sky had cleared and it was getting quite warm. It had been a hot late summer this year – a bit too hot for me. One of those where you just had to sit indoors and drink water or go swimming. One where it was too tiring to go out and be active.

Ellen must have thought I was crazy.

I could still hear her words, 'Why is it such a problem?' Why? I didn't want to think about why! It was bursting the bubble. The subject of my eyes was one that must be shut away or cried over in a fit of rage and then locked away again. Facing the issue wasn't an option.

How could I put it out of mind now? It was far too late. It was getting harder and harder to shut out the images of me in the future, and what it would be like if I didn't do something about my attitude.

The sea gulls were circling overhead. They all seemed to be shrieking it now. Why? Why? Why?

'I don't know!' I wanted to scream back at them.

Ellen's voice kept repeating in my head. 'I'm sorry, I don't see very well.' They were easy enough words to say, weren't they? I repeated them under my breath. I must have looked like I was praying or something. But even that whisper, which only I could hear, made me shrivel up inside.

'I don't know!' I raised my eyes to the sea gulls.

I was there for a long time until I had to walk back to Firtops to wait for Mum. How immature was I?! At 15 years old I still crumbled to pieces in the smallest difficult situation, and I still clung to the vain hope that one day I'd wake up and it would all magically have gone away.

What if I stayed forever like this? The image of sitting alone at that table in the day room, still pretending to be normal popped back into my mind. Crying whenever anyone reminded me that I couldn't see very well. I didn't like the conclusion I knew, and had always known, I would finally come to: Things were going to have to change.

Chapter 11

The next day I woke up, after sleeping intermittently, not looking forward at all to going to Firtops again. Although it hadn't been boring or gloomy as I'd expected, I was still nervous. I'd gone back to being shy of Ellen because of what had happened yesterday. Rain was hammering on my window and I opened the curtains and looked out. The street was all wet and somebody's gutter was dripping onto the pavement, loudly beside me. Autumn had definitely set in. The window had been open all night and now the whole room was chilly. I had to shut it quickly. My room was depressingly untidy I noticed for about the hundredth time, as I tripped over some clothes on the floor. The worse it got the harder it was to find motivation to tidy it. I stubbed my toe on something and picked it up. It's stupid to be angry with inanimate objects but I suppose you could describe it as human nature. Dad sometimes swore at the car because it wouldn't start and Mum was always saying how stupid the kettle was because you couldn't fill it up without unplugging it.

I bent to see what it was I'd hurt my toe on. It was a large dome-shaped magnifying glass. I'd wondered where that had got to. I was supposed to take it to school every day just in case the teachers had forgotten to enlarge anything for me, like that text book in History. I'd refused. It was huge and ugly and stupid-looking. It didn't help much anyway, though people with normal vision couldn't understand that. I'd pretended that it was broken so that I didn't have to bring it. It would take them ages to order a new one. Someone had asked me what it was once. I'd gone all hot and told them it was a paper weight. It was the same with a telescope I'd been given to allow me to read signs. Everyone would be staring at me if ever I bothered to use it. It made me look like a birdwatcher. Why would I be doing that at a train station? I hated it. Looking different, and in my opinion inferior, was the worst humiliation I could imagine. I'd surreptitiously left the telescope in our holiday chalet last summer. I dropped the magnifier on the floor, making it crash hard and Mark came in to ask what the noise was.

'Just some rubbish,' I said. A long crack had formed along the bottom of it. It was useless now. I shoved it in a bottom drawer, where all the things that I didn't know what to do with went.

This morning I was going to work with a man who lived a few flats along from Ellen, called James Darling. His bit of garden wasn't half as neat as hers. The lawn part was all long and straggly. Coming into the room I saw someone standing by what must be Mr. Darling's chair. When she turned and said hello I recognised her as Julia .There was loads of clutter on the floor. Magazines and newspapers lay on all the chairs and it smelt a bit neglected. I wondered why it wasn't cleaned more often and then it occurred to me that to be independent means having a choice in how often your room is cleaned.

'This is Mr. Darling, Louise,' said Julia quickly. She seemed busy, although it was still early in the day. I looked at the bald man sitting in the chair in front of me. He seemed tiny and shrivelled and frail; as though you could knock him over if you breathed too hard. His hands hung limply down by his sides and his stick legs poked out from his trousers. He looked like a doll.

'Sit down for a minute,' Julia continued. She seemed to be arranging his clothes on the tiny bed which stood behind us. There were two seats which were both piled high with papers. Cautiously I approached one of the chairs and scooped the pile up in my hands.

'Don't do that!'

His voice was thin and frail like his body, but sharp. It was all I could do to avoid dropping the papers on the floor in embarrassment. I put them carefully back down.

'Sorry.'

'I should think so too! Julia, who is this?'

'Oh dear. I forgot to introduce you didn't I? Mr Darling this is Louise. She's come to help us shopping.'

'Who said I needed any help?' I started at the sound of that familiar sentence. 'How old is she anyway?'

'I'm 15.'

Julia took forever lifting James into the wheelchair, and he wasn't afraid to make a fuss about it. 'I'm uncomfortable like this! The bar's digging into my back!' She seemed to know how to handle it and ignored him, almost as if he really was a doll. She just moved when he said 'move'. When at last we did get out it was raining fairly hard. I had to run back in for Mr. Darling's umbrella. Fortunately it was hanging on the arm of his chair. Why didn't it surprise me that I wasn't quick enough for his liking?

We walked to the town Shopping Centre without a word between us. The rain spattered on my and Julia's heads and we got splashed by the occasional car that passed by on the road to Haslecombe. My trousers were completely wet through by the time we came to the supermarket. We had to get some loo rolls, cigarettes, chocolate, a newspaper, about six hundred ready-meals and a six pack of Tetley's. He wasn't too happy about the fact that the beer had increased in price since he last came, and he didn't mind expressing his views for the whole shop to appreciate. I was mortified. I wondered why on earth I was needed here. Then I found out.

Julia leaned over to me behind his chair and handed me the bag of shopping.

'We need you to carry it because this isn't Mr. Darling's usual wheelchair. It's being mended and there isn't a board on the bottom of this one to hold things. He doesn't like to have shopping on his lap and I don't have a hand free. I would hang it on the handle but that would tip the whole thing up, so it's easier to have someone to carry it.' She turned to me and said in a low voice, 'Sorry I didn't have the chance to warn you beforehand.'

'What are you whispering about?' snapped Mr. Darling.

We started walking back as if he hadn't spoken, then I dropped the bag with the beer cans in because I tripped over a stone on the pavement.

'You idiot!' His forehead had huge frown lines down the middle and his mouth was gaping. 'When I open them they'll fizz everywhere and get me all wet.'

'Sorry.'

I turned away to hide my indignation. It was so strange that he should say that, when I was standing out here feeling like I'd been through the washing machine.

When we got back the cans had to be moved at least three times round the kitchen before they were in a satisfactory place. Even Julia, who seemed to have the power to ignore his bad temper, seemed a bit wound up. I was relieved when at last I was set free.

A well-meaning friend of Mum's once said that disabled people were different from everyone else. They were born with a special calm, caring attitude towards life and their situation. Perhaps she had said it to comfort me, but my own attitude had proved this theory wrong and James Darling had certainly reinforced it. It was gradually dawning on me that probably disability didn't determine an individual's personality at all. James would still grumble about everything even if he was able-bodied wouldn't he? And Ellen would certainly still be nice.

I was asked to see Ellen again next. I entered her room cautiously. I could see that her painting had come on quite a bit since yesterday. She was a fast worker. A big bright yellow sun hung in the white sky .She didn't mention what she'd said to me at all. I couldn't help watching her in admiration as she painted. Sometimes she'd drop the brush on the floor and have to bend to pick it up. I thought of going over and doing it for her, but then I thought of how I'd feel in that situation and stayed where I was. She spilt the paint water all over her skirt and I helped her to clear up the mess. I wondered what would have happened if James Darling had done that. It didn't bear thinking about.

I saw Nick again at lunch time. I could tell that we were going to be friends. I was very aware, however, that today Ellen was at the table with us, sitting opposite me. I'm sure she wasn't listening to any of the conversations around her. But it didn't seem anti-social. It was as if she was deep in thought about something. Sometimes she'd offer a comment to the lady sitting next to her. Nick was really easy to talk to. I finished my lunch way before he did, because he spent so much time chatting. We talked about all sorts. He was studying design technology at school and I told him how much I hated it.

'I'm hopeless at making things.' I said.

'I really enjoy it. It gives me a real sense of achievement. Not like in Maths and English'

'Not me', I thought. I had been awful at woodwork because I found it so difficult. Mrs. Philips would end up doing most of it for me, and she wasn't that great either.

'Haven't you got some sort of problem with your eyes?' He'd obviously decided that it was safe to ask. Or perhaps he hadn't even thought about it. Maybe it didn't seem like a sensitive question to him.

Ellen seemed to be looking at me now, engaged in what we were saying. Just at the wrong time!

'Yes,' I said.

'I've seen you around at school. You were in my DT class in year 7. Didn't you have that woman with you?'

He shoved a piece of pizza in his mouth, but I no longer had an appetite and that blushing had started.

'What is actually wrong with your eyes?....... That is, if it's not a rude question.'

I was blushing furiously now. Trying to swallow the potato that was in my mouth and sound cool and easy.

'No, no,' I stuttered. All I could see was Ellen's face.

'I had something called Retinoblastoma when I was a baby. It's...it's cancer.'

'Oh.'

There was an awkward silence. He was looking at me now and could see my distress.

'I haven't offended you have I?'

'No, not at all.'

'Can you pass me the salt please?' It was Ellen. I obliged. 'I was just thinking about my next painting. I think I'll do a portrait. I haven't done one for a long time. I hope I haven't lost the knack. Mind you, it might be difficult to find somebody willing to sit for me that long.' And she sprinkled the salt onto her potato.

'Who is this young man?'

'I'm Nick.'

'Are you doing work experience here as well, Nick?'

'Yeah. Not what you'd expect, is it?'

'Oh, I'm sure you're getting on very well! Louise is, aren't you Louise? What subjects do you do at school?'

And I realised that she hadn't been listening to a word we'd said.

Somehow Nick and I got to talking about our plans for the evening. I told him that I'd have to wait here for my Mum to finish work.

'Well, if you've got time on your hands, how do you fancy going somewhere after we've done here? I make my own way home, you see, and I sometimes spend a bit of time in town first.'

We ended up in this little Cafe near the harbour. I'd been there a couple of times with Naomi and a few other friends. It was good with Nick. He was careful with me. Perhaps too careful, but that didn't matter. He'd learn in time what I could and couldn't see. He didn't say things like. 'I'll look that way and you look this way,' at road sides. He was like David in that respect. For the first time it was clear that admitting that I had a sight problem made things easier.

We chatted about anything and everything. He was into music and played the guitar. I found myself laughing a lot that evening. I wasn't shy of him at all by now and I knew it was because he wasn't at all shy himself. He drew me out of myself with his chatty nature. We seemed to spend hours in that Cafe, talking and looking out at the sea, which raged out of the window. They made great hot chocolate here. Nice and creamy. Not like that muddy water you get out of packets. There were lovely caramel slices and muffins that were too huge to manage alone. I'd have to come here again.

'I've really enjoyed today,' he said. 'We'll have to do it again sometime.'

I was feeling fantastic by now. Mum was cross because I was late for meeting her. It sounds stupid, but that felt really good, going out and having fun rather than wallowing in my constant self-pity.

Chapter 12

After work at Firtops next day I came across Craig in Haslecombe. I had decided always to go there now while I was waiting to be picked up. It had been a long day and I was really tired, more so than on a school day and I'd spent some of it with darling James Darling which didn't help. It had been much warmer than yesterday and he'd wanted me to open windows and then close them again whenever a slight breeze blew. I'd spoken to Ellen about him. The worry that she might confront me with problems that I was too weak to face was gone. I knew her well enough now to realise that she wouldn't push me into anything. In a weird way I wished she would. I didn't have the power myself to face facts so perhaps if somebody did it for me things would be easier. Hadn't David done just that in the History lesson though? It'd suddenly become clear that maybe his motives hadn't been for Becky's sake after all. Maybe he was trying to help me.

I thought about my future all the time now. There was no going back and being naïve anymore; I was beginning to open my eyes to the world. I knew that soon things would have to change and I really would have to grow up. Was I starting to see my actions in a new light? Admittedly I'd never been able to justify the way I was so stubborn, I'd just let myself forget, but things were moving on and I had to run to keep up. I kept thinking about all the things that I'd be expected to be able to do in a few years. Get around, get a job, keep a house. Even go to university. The bubble had to burst whether I was prepared for it or not. The world wasn't designed for me and people like me, so I was going to have to adjust to it. I was pleased with what I'd managed to do yesterday. I'd actually admitted about myself without too much trouble and it had made things better, not worse. Nick hadn't looked down on me for it had he? Plus I'd done it alone. Ellen hadn't even been listening. For the first time I was proud of myself. This was the start.

I was hanging around the harbour again eating fish and chips because Mum and Dad were going out that night and I couldn't be bothered to make myself anything – or I didn't have the ability. I pretended that I could've cooked if I'd wanted to, but it usually ended with me opening a packet. Even then it was only if I was familiar with the instructions, or Mum was around to ask. It was ridiculous, the amount of space on the back of packets, compared to the amount they used for their tiny writing.

I heard the voice and then saw him. He was with a little boy and they were play-fighting. He was heading in my direction. I'd just about managed to forget about him for the time being, what with being so busy with Firtops, and I waited for all that humiliation to come flooding back on seeing him, but where was that stomach jolt?

'Louise,' Craig said, noticing me. I was a little overwhelmed, but where were the visions of me sliding on the ice and the frustration? I was still a bit shy, probably because I didn't know him that well, but not embarrassed.

'Hello Craig.'

'I see you've had the sling taken off.'

'Yeah. It's all better now.'

'Listen.......' he said and stopped. He opened his mouth to continue but closed it again. The wind tugged at his T shirt.

'How's work experience? Where've you been placed?'

'Firtops. How about you?'

'I'm helping at a DIY store. Not much fun. See you around yeah?'

'Sure.'

He began to talk quickly.

'I've been wanting to say this for ages … but I suppose I haven't had the chance…'

My heart was fast. To my utter amazement, all I could think was; 'Please don't ask me out, please, no.'

He was really agitated. I suppose it was out of character for someone like him to be talking, as he was, to someone like me.

'I'm really sorry about that time on the ice rink… I really upset you… I never meant to do that… I'm always shooting my mouth off… anyone'll tell you that…'

'Don't worry about it.' I was too taken aback to say anything else. Was this the same person? He was actually being sensitive to my feelings.

I watched, astounded, until he disappeared. Why hadn't I felt that rush when I'd heard him call my name? Why wasn't I feeling that tingly excitement? He'd come up to talk to me without invitation. I thought about when he did that on the ice just before 'the incident.' How great I'd felt that he should be in a crowd and call out to me specifically. But, just now, when I'd thought he was going to ask me out, I'd felt terrible. That was supposed to be my dream wasn't it?

It took me quite a while to work it out. I was sitting up in bed sipping a hot chocolate as it was cold tonight. I'd just finished reading my book. I only managed about a chapter at a time before my eyes got tired. Sometimes I still had my parents read to me and I'd had books on tape in the past. I was just thinking about how normal people sometimes got books on tape so it had to be all right to get another one, and then I reminded myself of my latest thoughts on this issue. I wasn't 'normal' and I was going to have to face it. There was no going back now. I wasn't a child any more.

What had happened today with Craig? It felt so sudden and strange, not to have all those feelings of excitement about him. I couldn't believe that I'd actually hoped that he wouldn't ask me out.

I tried to recall imagining skating into his arms again. But nothing happened. There was nothing there at all, no wish that it could all come true. I knew, once and for all that I no longer fancied him and, in a strange way, I was glad. It would make my life a lot easier. But I felt like something was missing now. This had been going on for so long, and now that it had finished I realised just how much I'd miss it.

Chapter 13

I lay awake for hours with the radio on: not too loudly so as not to wake anyone up. They played loads of soppy romantic songs at this time of night. I realised that tears were in my eyes, but not because of the music. The question was in my mind again; why couldn't I tell anybody that I couldn't see? Loads of people had disabilities didn't they? It wasn't anything to be ashamed of. It was frustrating and annoying but not my fault. It wasn't as if I'd committed a crime. It was so difficult to believe though, when in my everyday life I was faced with people who had this gift. Where were all the other partially sighted people in the world? They didn't spend all their time in hospitals. It was a constant 'them' and 'me' situation. But again, I felt guilty. If I was ashamed of my disability wasn't it like saying that people in wheelchairs, people like Ellen should be ashamed too? It was like Hitler or something; obsession with being physically perfect.

One of the best parts about being friends with Nick was that there was no chance of there being a Craig incident. He knew, just like David knew, and I could be myself easily. I didn't have to try to be normal so much, I could just be normal but without the lying. It was much better to have friends like that. I had loved it when he said he admired me. I'd never had anyone say that to me before. I'd handled my problem pretty badly, but I supposed that if I learnt to cope (and I knew that I'd have to sooner or later or end up like Mr Darling), then perhaps I would be worthy of some admiration.

I was in a good mood next morning even though I hadn't had much sleep. I'd put worrying about the future to one side for the time being. There was nothing I could do immediately was there? There was my work experience to finish, and my coursework and revision for GCSEs to get done. Maybe it was because the pain of 'the incident' was officially healed and Craig was no longer on my mind, that I felt better. I could tell mum had noticed and she must have been glad. I'd been so low lately.

It was a miserable day again; raining really heavily and dull and dark. The days were getting shorter and sometimes the smell of autumn bonfires would be on the wind. I loved that smell.

There was something distinctly different about Firtops today. I noticed that from the very start. It was in the way people spoke and acted. Mrs Symonds greeted me, as she always did in the mornings when I came into the entrance hall to ask what to do, but there was definitely something more pressing on her mind. She seemed flustered and eventually gave me laundry duty, and I groaned inwardly. She spoke more quickly, and was more distant than usual. There was something tense and anxious about her. I wondered if she had a problem at home.

Some people drifted into the hall from a side door. They seemed to want to speak to Mrs Symonds and I sensed that I was making this a problem. What had happened? Was there some secret? Perhaps somebody had died or something. Or a fire in one of the bungalows last night maybe. Had I done something wrong? I felt uncomfortable.

I had to help bring in some washing off the line which had been left out by mistake. It was still drizzling as I squelched through the mud. Typically, it was the line right at the back of the area by the fence, that was still covered in dripping bed sheets. When bringing them back, I realised that one was dragging through the mud and would have to go through the wash again. There were more people than usual in the laundry room. It wasn't very big. There were only three washing machines, a couple of dryers, an indoor line and some wicker chairs. The room was quite cluttered, like an overfilled lift, with six or so women who were leaning on the various machines or sitting in their wheelchairs. I had to dodge through them to get to the washing machine, which wasn't easy. I made for the one with the digital dial; the only one I could read. There was a lady sitting right in front of it in her chair who told me to 'use the other one.' I shrugged it off as best I could, and told her some pathetic lie about how I'd been told specifically by a Carer that I should use this one. Things were always so much easier in theory than in real life!

Everyone here seemed extra talkative as well. I tried to eavesdrop to find out what was going on, but there were too many different conversations so I didn't take much notice of it. It could just be the rain causing boredom and restlessness, like wet break time at infant school. Maybe there was nothing good on TV.

It was Edith who eventually enlightened me. She was the sort of person who spent most of her time gossiping in the day room, just as she was doing now; some of my friends were like that. She liked a good story and her voice was full of excitement as she feverishly folded her flowery aprons.

'I say, Louise,' she said, seeing me clumsily trying to battle my way through the wheelchair army. I'd helped her do some dusting yesterday afternoon. She hadn't stopped harping on all the time I was there. Not that I'd minded; at least she was friendly.

'Do you know that young lad? Is he from your school?'

Did she mean Nick?

'The boy on work experience?'

'Yes...... what's his name?'

'Nick.'

'Imagine the cheek of that boy!'

I stopped loading washing into the machine, and turned around. What was she talking about? What was Nick supposed to have done?

'What?'

'You haven't heard! Oh poor girl. I hope you weren't too fond of the young lad. Mind you, they can be very deceptive.'

There was something almost teasing in her voice.

'What's he done?' I was slightly annoyed already, by the fact that none of them seemed to be moving out of my way as I tried to reach for the washing basket. And I was now very bewildered.

'Oh you tell her Elizabeth.' Edith was in a big flap now. It seemed as if she was enjoying herself. 'I have to relate the story to Teresa. Dear Tess, she'll be so upset.'

I looked at Elizabeth intently as Edith disappeared out of the door, calling Tess down the corridor.

'Sorry, Louise,' said Elizabeth. 'Edith isn't very good at making sense at times like this. She does get so agitated.'

'What's wrong? What's happened?'

'It's that Nick boy.'

'Yes?'

'He's supposed to have done a bad thing.' I was really getting wound up now! A bad thing?

'What?'

'It's to do with that James Darling... typical really I suppose...'

'What? What about James Darling?' What was Nick supposed to have done? Murdered him? I wouldn't blame him! Elizabeth seemed slightly taken aback at the tone of my voice. I wasn't talking in my usual polite, carefully prepared way.

'Nick was helping him to clean his flat yesterday and old James says he pinched his wallet.'

'That's ridiculous! Nick would never do something like that!'

'Oh dear! You are fond of him aren't you? I find it very hard to believe myself, but it's true you never know people as well as you think.'

'Everyone knows what a ... misery James is!'

Someone tutted sympathetically.

My legs gave way and I had to sit on one of the wicker chairs that was already piled high with washing. It was a good job that was where I happened to be standing, or I could have ended up in one of their laps. I was horrified!

'W-why do they think it was Nick?' My voice was faint.

'Julia had gone to get some more cleaning cloths so James and Nick were alone in James's room. He saw Nick taking something off his chest of drawers and later found that his wallet was missing, and it's nowhere to be found.'

'It must have fallen onto the floor or something.'

'Oh no, that's what we all hoped, because we're all fond of Nick. They would've found it wouldn't they? They've done a thorough check all over the place.'

'And he's sure it was Nick?'

'I hate to say this, Louise. We all know James Darling is a lot of things but he's as honest as the day is long.'

'Where's Nick now?'

'He's waiting for his mother to come and pick him up.'

I asked the Carer who had just come in if it was OK to go to the loo. I had to find Nick.

He was sitting in the entrance hall; one of the first places I looked. He seemed distressed and pale, nothing like his usual self.

'Louise,' he spoke quietly because people were sitting behind the reception desk at the far end of the room. There was something desperate in his voice. It sounded almost like James's Darling's. Thin and choked.

'You've heard then?'

I nodded.

'Who told you?'

'Edith.'

He had his chin in his hands and his elbows on his knees, looking hunched and anxious.

'And do you believe her?' he demanded, almost disgusted. We'd talked about Edith the other day. We'd laughed about how exaggerated everything she said seemed to be, and how 'over the top' she was.

'Well... No.' My thoughts were in turmoil. One minute I'd been fighting my way through laundry land on a normal, if a little dreary, day, and now this.

'I didn't... do anything.' He was trying to look at me.

I had to leave him at this point, making a faint excuse about how they'd be missing me. I needed time alone to think.

'Oh thanks a lot Louise!' I heard his voice behind me as I walked off down the corridor. I half-turned round, but he was heading out of the door with his mum, who must have had to take time out of work. She was talking angrily to someone who was evidently a staff member.

There was nothing else on my mind for the whole of the rest of the day. James Darling was certainly an old misery, but so many people, who knew him really well, said that, if anything, he was too honest. By lunch time I'd come to the sad conclusion that it must be true. The world was turned upside down and Nick wasn't who I'd thought he was. Like with Craig on the ice. Why did things always go wrong for me? Why weren't things simple like they seemed to be for all my friends? Just a life of finding boyfriends and going out for a laugh; never having any serious concerns. Then all through lunch I couldn't help thinking of Nick's witty personality, the way we'd become friends so quickly. He was so nice! Could he really sink that low? And who should I trust? A load of people I hardly knew or someone I was beginning to think of as one of my best friends?

I helped Ellen in the afternoon. She knew that something was up and had guessed how I was feeling. She was getting to know me so well.

'You've heard the news, then?'

'Yes.'

'You really like that boy, don't you? I saw you talking a couple of times. I like him too. Really nice lad. He helped me with painting only yesterday morning. Wouldn't stop talking. I didn't get very much done. Cheerful personality. But James couldn't be lying. He doesn't lie. Too honest for his own good, sometimes. Poor old Elizabeth got her glasses just the other week and he wasn't afraid to tell her what he thought of them. And all the ladies get to know if they've put on weight!' She chuckled. Usually I'd join in, but I couldn't stop my thinking.

'Apparently James only picked up his pension from the Post Office yesterday and put it all in his wallet. The Carers know he always keeps it in the same drawer, I hope there's another explanation. I really do. I can hardly believe it of the boy either.'

Did she realise just how much I hoped so too?

I was with Mr Darling in the afternoon. It was really unfair of them to put me there today! And how could they trust me if they didn't trust Nick? Of course I felt extra bitter towards James. It was nearly impossible to stop myself from biting back when he made a rude remark. He was still in bed because he was feeling a bit off-colour. Someone had brought his lunch in for him today.

'And anyway, what are you doing here at the weekend?' he snapped, just as Julia walked into the room.

'Mr Darling, you haven't touched your lunch,' she said.

'Don't fancy it,' he growled. 'Take it away!'

Without a word Julia picked up the tray and walked out of the door with it. I quickly followed her.

'Did you hear that? He doesn't even know what day it is! How could he know where he put that wallet?' It was very out of character for me to put forward an argument like this, but here was something I felt strongly about.

'Oh, Louise. Nick's your friend. It's natural for you to want to find excuses, but I'm afraid that, in this instance, there just aren't any. Nick was in the room and the wallet was there. I left, and when I came back the wallet was gone and so was he, supposedly to do a job for somebody else. It's as simple as that.'

Suddenly it occurred to me that perhaps she was the one who was lying. Who were people more likely to suspect? A woman who'd been working with them for years or an inexperienced schoolboy who they didn't know? I was on the verge of accusing her there and then when I realised how ridiculous and dangerous that would be.

I wanted to slap James's silly bald head. I hated him more than ever.

I just couldn't work it out. I found myself at the harbour after work again, upset because I'd hoped, on the way to work, that Nick and I would go somewhere together. I walked past the cafe that we'd been in. At last I was on my own, to think properly. What had he done?! If he really had stolen the money, then why? Surely he'd realise he'd be found out! I tried to remember things he'd said about himself. He'd told me he had a Saturday job in a supermarket. He'd said something about his Dad being out of work. Perhaps he had a good reason for doing it. I had to excuse his actions. He was too nice, too light-hearted for me to believe something like this. But maybe he'd been trying to fool me so that I'd believe his story. He could have been planning it all along. Maybe it had only been a joke. To spite Mr Darling? Not a very funny one!

I wondered what would happen to Nick. Would he be taken to court? Maybe he'd just own up. If he did, then would I ever be able to be his friend again? Could I ever trust him? It was hard to believe that I'd only known him for a few days. I really didn't know that much about him. I'd never even been to his house. Why was somebody who I'd known for such a short time having such an impact on me?

I rang up Catherine that night, then Naomi and then David. I didn't tell any of them about it. We talked about how work experience was going and how we should all meet up sometime.

I needed to get back to the old life and my old friends and pretend I hadn't been faced with this. It had really thrown me.

David had had a fight with Becky. I knew he was distraught, but he tried to hide it.

'I don't know what went wrong. She just came round the other afternoon and we were at each other's throats all day.'

'Maybe she's not who you think she is,' I said cryptically

'What do you mean?'

'I don't know. Perhaps she's met someone else.'

Looking back that wasn't a particularly tactful thing to say. I couldn't concentrate on his problems right now, so how could I expect him to always be attentive and sensitive to mine? I wasn't being much of a friend. We decided to go somewhere together to take his mind off it. I tried not to think about Nick. That was the only way to handle it at the moment. I had been thinking about him constantly and it wasn't doing me any good.

Chapter 14

At last it was the final day of work experience. I was more relieved than I'd expected to be because, up until the problems with Nick had happened, I'd begun to enjoy being there. Even though going back to school seemed like a dreary prospect, at least it was ordinary and I'd know what to expect every day. School was also a place where I could lose myself, even if it was in boring work. I wouldn't see Nick and I wouldn't have to think about what he might have done. I tried to ignore the fact that there was no Nick at lunch time. I sat next to Ellen and talked to her instead. She could tell that I was upset about it all.

It pounded with rain all day. I had to water the plants in the little conservatory and I could hardly hear myself think, with the noise of it spattering overhead. It was cosy I suppose. I felt like I was somewhere tropical. Some of the plants had really huge leaves that I had to push through to get to the pot to pour the water in. If I ever got rich I decided that I'd have one of these on the back of my million pound mansion. I wondered what Nick was doing now. Probably at home. Perhaps he was even still in bed. He might enjoy not having to do anything. A bit like a holiday? No, of course not.

I was with Ellen all afternoon. She'd completed her masterpiece now. She encouraged me to look at it with my nose nearly touching it and I almost laughed as I thanked her; at how much I'd moved my head around whilst standing so close to it, as if I was an art critic or something! The picture was amazing! A green field full of daffodils with a bright springtime sky overhead.

'That would brighten up any room,' I said. 'Just looking at it reminds me of the spring.'

'Thank you Louise. We'll just have to see what the local gallery thinks of it, won't we?'

'I'd buy it if I had the money.'

As usual I watched her paint. Today she was putting in the finishing touches. I began to think about my eyes again. I had managed to mostly forget for the past day or so. For once I had been caught up in somebody else's problems rather than my own. It was Ellen who'd first started me thinking and worrying about getting out of this trap by making me face up to it. It was like a cloud that loomed over me. I had mixed emotions whenever I saw her. She made me feel good about myself because she was cheerful and positive about life, but at the same time I knew that I was being really weak compared to her. We sat in silence. The silences weren't awkward at all now. I expect she enjoyed having the space to think. What sort of things did she think about?

I had plenty of time for my own thoughts. I could see in my head all sorts of occasions such as that maths lesson where I'd done no work. There'd been loads of times like that. How ridiculous I'd been to let that happen! How silly my actions were. Seeing Mr Darling worried me too. I'd been trying to avoid thinking about it but I knew it was often at the back of my mind that I could well have a disposition like his in my old age.

My birthday wasn't so far away. Deep admiration for Ellen engulfed me again as I looked at her broken little body and I wondered what her life had been like when she was younger. She suddenly looked up from swirling the blue-tipped brush.

'I'll miss you, you know.'

'Me too.'

'You're my only way of keeping in touch with the youngsters these days.' She laughed her running water laugh.

'You're a real inspiration Ellen,' I stammered. I was blushing and very self-conscious. It was only very occasionally that I aired deep feelings like that.

'I hope I've helped you. I'm lucky you know, Louise. My disability is something I can't hide. Well unless I wore an extra big dress.' Once more she was joking about it.

'But you. It's much harder with you. It's in your hands whether or not you talk about it.' I expect she'd wanted to say these things ever since I'd met her.

'Folk take me or leave me. They see me as I am. You have to be a lot braver. People don't consider the fact that it might be hard in that respect do they?'

I shook my head. I felt a bit uncomfortable in spite of myself. Would I be able to see Ellen again? The thought that I might not shocked me.

'Be strong Louise.' I felt as if I was about to cry, but there was no anger, or even proper sadness. I knew just where she was coming from.

'You know you can come and see me whenever you like.'

'Thanks.'

'If ever you want to chat. Not that I'm the most interesting of your friends to chat to.'

I liked that. She called herself my friend and of course she was interesting!

At the end of the day when I was going to sign out there were loads of people standing in the entrance hall as I came through the heavy wooden door to the side. What was it all about this time? Was there news of Nick?

They all turned to face me and I shuddered with nerves. What had I done? It wasn't until I saw the expressions on their faces as I drew much closer that I realised. They were all smiling at me. Lots of the residents and some of the staff, with Ellen sitting in their midst in today's blue dress and Mrs Symonds standing behind her.

'Louise,' said Mrs Symonds. 'We couldn't let you go without saying good-bye.'

'You've been a great help to us all, especially me,' said Ellen.

'So we all signed this card for you.' It was Edith. The organiser. A big card with a vase of flowers painted on the front was handed to me with signatures and messages in it. I expected only to be able to read half of them but they were all written in large, even writing. I wondered whose doing that was. I felt that stomach jolt for a few moments. They must all know about me. But they were all offering their thanks for the various cleaning or services I'd done for them.

'Thank you for your support.' 'You're a lovely girl.' 'Do come and visit us sometimes.' I was surprised at being able to read all the handwriting. It was like the way the teachers did it for me at school.

'You've been really helpful.'

For once I was content to be the centre of attention. I basked in their praises and let them know how much I'd miss them. Even if I had only been there for a week.

But I couldn't help thinking of Nick. He was supposed to be here too, wasn't he? I knew he'd spent hours in the sodden garden digging weeds and planting out new things for the spring. I wondered again where he was at the moment. Probably at home in front of the TV, wasting away the hours.

Of course they expected a bit of a speech, which completely threw me. We'd all moved into the day-room and they were sitting in the chairs around the tables with me standing among them. Silence fell. All eyes must be on me now.

'I just want to say, then,' I began. Frantically searching for words.

'It's been a really fun week and I've enjoyed being with you all. I must admit that I've had my views about Residential Care Homes changed dramatically.' They all laughed. I felt like the best man at a wedding.

As I was about to leave, Mrs Symonds caught me.

'Well done, Louise. You've been great. Perhaps we could give you a summer job here or something.' I'd wanted a job of some sort and they all knew what I could manage here.

'Oh and before you go,' she continued. 'You got on rather well with Ellen didn't you?' 'I wonder if you'd like to come to a surprise birthday party for her. She's always talking about you, you know. That lady's got a soft spot for you.'

I went out with some friends on Friday evening. We saw a film. It was complete rubbish but that didn't matter. We all had a laugh. It was a bit of a party in itself; to celebrate the end of the work experience week. We went back to Naomi's house and we spent the whole evening exchanging stories.

'How did Nick get on? He was with you wasn't he? He left early didn't he?' I felt myself grow hot, but somehow managed to keep my voice almost casual as I said, 'Yeah, fine. I think he was ill.'

Catherine had been to a vet's where she'd spent the whole time cleaning instruments, except occasionally there'd been an animal that she had to hold.

'This bloke came in with a parrot. He was all smart, wearing a suit and that. And the parrot kept shouting 'bloody hell' and 'piss off' and stuff like that. It was well funny.'

'Well I was in a First School,' said Naomi. She'd always been interested in working with children. 'Once we were playing I Spy. This little boy said something beginning with 'ch'. So we were all guessing, you know, 'chair', 'chocolate'... we even tried 'chicken'. And at last he had to tell us... 'chree'.'

'Chree?!'

'Y'know, conkers grow on them.'

'He was so sweet!' She had lots of stories about the little kids. She was good at telling them too. I'd never really been very good with children. What were you supposed to say to them? Also it was very hard for me to 'keep an eye' on them. That would mean I'd have to follow them over adventure playgrounds.

'Have you heard about Becky?' It was Georgina, Becky's best friend. 'Oh you probably have, Louise. You're mates with David aren't you.'

'No. I mean, no I haven't 'heard''.

'Becky dumped him.'

'Why?' It was Catherine, not me. I was too busy gaping. David had only told me they'd been having problems.

'I don't know. Apparently it just wasn't working or whatever.'

I felt guilty now. For ignoring him and not seeming very interested when he'd phoned me.

'Were they having arguments?' This time it was me. I'd found words.

'Were they ever! I went out shopping in Haslecombe the other day and everything they said to each other seemed to be the wrong thing.'

'Do you think it's another woman?' said Naomi. I'd never have said something like that. She was half joking. It must all be Becky's fault. I knew how much she meant to David. He was always going on about her.

'I don't think so. It's not very 'Davidish' is it? Anyway, it only happened the other day, so I haven't managed to get all the gossip.'

I wasn't sure that I wanted to hear 'the gossip.' I'd always wondered if Becky was right for David and I'd tried to tell him. Still, I wouldn't go on about it too much I decided. He'd be too upset.

When I got home I had to phone him.

'Believe me Lou, you wouldn't understand. Just trust me when I say that it wasn't her fault. Let's not go into it.'

He sounded really gutted.

'Can I tell you something?'

'Yeah, of course.'

'Promise not to tell anyone, it wouldn't be fair on him.'

'On who?'

'Promise not to tell.'

'Oh come on, Louise, what do you take me for?'

'Do you know Nick Summers?'

'Yeah, he's in my Maths class.'

'He was doing work experience with me.'

'Do I sense romance?' he said in his usual buoyant way, but he sounded rather gloomy. I laughed anyway. Why did him saying that embarrass me? And why had I lied to my friends about it?

'He's been accused of stealing one of the resident's wallets.'

'No way! Has he been prosecuted?'

I felt that jolt in my stomach again. That could really happen, couldn't it?

'How well do you know him? Is he nice?' I said, in a shaky voice.

'Seems to be, but he can't be that nice can he?'

'I'm kind of hoping that there's some alternative explanation for all of this.' And I still was. More so than ever.

'Are you sure you don't fancy him?'

'Yes!' I said, laughing again and blushing.

David and I went to the park on Saturday. It was nice to be spending time with him again, although I knew how selfish that was. No Becky tagging along. We collected conkers like we used to. There weren't many good ones left. All the little boys must've taken them already. Then we had a leaf fight, like in the old days. Covering each other in the last of the dying, brittle leaves. Our jeans got soaked on the muddy ground. I could see that David hadn't gelled his hair that morning and it kept flying in tangled strands all over his face. It was great to hear him laughing again.

I think we laughed a bit too hard because we got grumbled at by an old man walking his scruffy little dog, which made us laugh even more. I'd heard that yappy little dog around the village before, and the man often made irritating comments. Mr Darling's brother maybe?!

'This is a public place!' he shouted at us. We tried to look serious. We couldn't look at each other.

'You're making such a racket.' The dog started to yap again, drowning out whatever he was droning on about now.

'Speak for yourself!' said David under his breath. We walked away in fits of laughter, feeling and sounding like two kids.

Later on I tried to talk to him about Nick. He seemed a bit offhand. He must be thinking of Becky.

Chapter 15

'Louise, how are you doing?' Stupidly, I didn't know who it could be at first. It made me jump to hear his voice. I wanted him to speak more.

'I'm OK.'

'How was the end of work experience?'

I felt awkward and guilty. I hadn't even had the guts to phone him. His voice was slightly forced.

'All right. What about you? Are you OK?' I was suddenly a bit shy with Nick. I never had been before. He was the kind of person that it's almost impossible to be shy with. But I was managing it.

'Why are you calling me?' I had to ask. What did he want? How could I be friends with somebody who I hadn't been supporting in a tough time and who I didn't quite trust anyway? And, even if I was wrong, I was being horrible. I'd been thinking that our friendship would have to be forgotten. I didn't know him well enough to be sure of him, to always know he was telling the truth and stick by him.

'I have to convince you that I didn't take that wallet. You still don't believe me, do you?'

'I really want to, of course I want to… but how can I? You have to admit that all the evidence is against you.'

'I don't know what really happened. All I know is that it wasn't me. This is serious, you know. The Police came round and they've decided not to prosecute me, thank God, because they obviously didn't find the wallet. I still won't get a good report and it'll look bad on my CV.'

'What are you going to do?'

'Keep telling them I didn't do it. What else can I do?'

'If it was you… it would be better if you confessed it.'

Even before the words were out of my mouth, I wanted to take them back. I heard a click at the other end of the line. I stood by the phone for some minutes, wondering what to do. How would I feel if I was accused like this? If I hadn't done it? That in itself would be bad enough, but if none of my friends believed me either... Should I ring him back? Give him the benefit of the doubt? He would probably be really angry with me, and who could blame him?

With shaky fingers I dialled the number.

'I'm sorry. You must be going through hell at the moment.'

'You're bloody right I am! You've got to understand how I feel… I need you to believe me.'

'Shall we meet up sometime?' He needed his friends. Did any of the others believe him?

'Haven't told them. They'll find out soon enough though, won't they? It seems like Mum's the only one on my side here,' he said when I asked him.

'And me,' I said, quietly.

So we agreed to meet.

It was Ellen's birthday party on Saturday. I wondered how old she actually was going to be. I felt that I knew her so well, but in reality, I knew hardly anything about her. I was curious about her past. What she'd done throughout her life, and how she'd come to be at Firtops. I went round there at ten. There was still frost on the grass when I arrived. The big white house was glistening in the winter sun, looking like some kind of Russian palace. The orangey sunlight was just behind it, making it look as if it was on fire, yet ice hung in the sharp air. It would make a lovely painting. I'd mention it to Ellen.

The party was held in the day-room. Lots of paintings, which must have been done by Ellen, were displayed on the walls. I talked to her for a while in the morning, noticing that she seemed tired but pleased to see me. The party was very successful and afterwards they all sang songs around the old piano. Ones that you'd expect to hear on an old black and white film. I knew some of them but was too shy to join in. I kind of murmured under my breath until Mary persuaded me to do a duet with Ellen. My self-consciousness was soon gone. Singing with Ellen was an amazing thing to do! It was as if I was trying to share my tiny bit of talent with her. I was even congratulated on my voice! Ellen had a nice voice as well, despite what she'd said. She got everyone to sing a couple of hymns, including her favourite; 'How Great Thou Art'

It had taken a lot of thought to decide what to get her for a present. She was even more difficult to consider than my Dad, who usually ended up with a couple of pairs of socks or some after-shave. I'd found a little shop in Haslecombe High Street, which I'd never really paid much attention to before. It was one of those tiny, dark places that looked as if it used to be somebody's front room. It was Mum who suggested that I had a look for a present in there. Inside it sold candles and little trinkets and it smelt of bubble bath. I bought a picture frame with daisies all around the edge. Maybe Ellen could put it on the chest of drawers with all the others. At first I couldn't decide whether or not she'd think it was tacky. But she always seemed to have flowers of some kind on her television, even if they weren't real.

She kept saying how lovely it was and picking it up to admire it. She was a popular lady; she knew what to say to everyone, but I'm sure she genuinely liked my little present. She was animated and upbeat all afternoon. There was an excited glow about her, and a huge, very obvious beam on her face.

I went to the back of the room to get a drink from the table I'd been directed to. There was Mr Darling, sitting on his own. He was in a corner of the room, his hands sagging down by his sides, a very miserable look on his face. If I'd felt more charitable towards him I would have said he was just tired. I wanted to hate him, more than ever now, but a part of me felt sorry for him. I wondered why he he'd been invited; I don't suppose he'd spoken to Ellen much over the years, except to complain about something. But then it wasn't fair to leave people out of occasions like this.

Nick should've been here too.

I really did feel I was useful to the staff that day. They treated me like one of them, asking me to restock the biscuits tray and make endless pots of tea. Then, suddenly out of the blue, after the party had finished and I was helping to wash up, Mr Darling said that his bin needed emptying. I was the one asked to grant his wish, because everyone was so busy. I took my yellow-gloved hands out of the sink. I'd tried to avoid thinking about James all afternoon and could easily have said no to him, now that I wasn't officially working here anymore. But I went reluctantly with him to his room. I followed him closely across the lawns and, unusually, he didn't say a word. The room was in a right mess, with old men's shirts and trousers all over the bed. The usual papers were piled high on the chairs. What were they all? Bills? Letters of complaint? He'd obviously taken time deciding what to wear today. A comb lay on the table beside his chair. Well I suppose he did have a few hairs in a fringe at the back of his head. He must have taken lots of care over his appearance. For a moment I began to realise that he was human and again I felt a spark of sympathy, but quickly brushed the thought aside.

'I've never seen you before! You must be new here. The bin's over there. Somehow or another it got knocked over and there's rubbish all over the floor under the dresser. When it's done you need to take it to the bin place.'

'Where's that?' I asked, expecting some kind of aggressive answer.

'It's behind the....No. In front of the...Oh you must know! You're obviously a new member of staff. Haven't they shown you round?'

I could see what he meant about the rubbish!

'It was only emptied this morning...or was it yesterday. Actually it was 3 days ago wasn't it...?' He was talking to himself now! This wasn't like him! He hadn't even remembered who I was!

You must have guessed what I was thinking. The scenes going through my head of finding his wretched wallet squashed behind the dresser. Of me pulling it out and presenting it to him. Him going, 'oh' as I proved that Nick was no thief. I allowed myself to imagine Nick and me laughing. Maybe my being sent here today was fate! How many normal people ask for their bins to be emptied when everyone's at a party?

Of course there was nothing there really. Finally all the rubbish was collected into a plastic bag that I'd somehow managed to find and I picked it up, ready to head off to the party again to ask where the dustbins were and get out of there as quickly as possible. It was uncomfortable being with him. I still couldn't help thinking that this could be the future me if my attitude didn't change. He'd turned the TV on and the 6 o' clock news was blaring from the corner of the room. He started grumbling about his 'thumping head' and was rummaging around for some paracetamol in the drawer beside me.

I stared at the chest for a minute, imagining Nick cleaning it, finding the wallet, then slipping it quickly and silently into his jacket pocket? No, there had to be some other explanation. The chest was a bit like Ellen's, but not so intricate. I was glad about that. I wanted everything about Mr Darling to be bad.

'What do you think you're doing?' The sound of his sharp voice had made me jump. I whirled around to face him in the dingy shadow at the back of the room, more annoyed than I should have been. I couldn't even empty a bin to his satisfaction.

'What?' There was a ring of irritation in my voice, even though I'd long learnt that he was best ignored when he got like this.

'Oh I get it,' he said and snatched up a small piece of paper from in front of me. 'You've been reading this haven't you?' He waved the paper in my face. It had been lying on the dark wooden surface of the dresser. I hadn't even noticed it. There were photos on the dresser as well. People in uniform.

'What?'

'It's you, isn't it?'

'I beg your pardon?'

'I haven't seen my wallet for a long time and I know I didn't just lose it! You've got it haven't you? I remember you were here when it went missing and this is the bank statement! Yes. You want to see how much there is.' He spoke like they do on detective programmes, when they suddenly discover the key to the mystery.

'I don't know what you're talking about.' I felt hot and flustered. I knew I was blushing.

'This is what I'm talking about.' He handed the paper to me. Tiny faint letters were printed on it like on a receipt.

'I have lots of money and you were trying to see how much there is! You were reading this and you thought that I was too stupid to notice. Well I'm not stupid my girl. Not me!'

I had a wild desire to shout back at him, 'Yes you are!'

'No! I wasn't reading anything!'

'Don't get stroppy with me, love.' I'd never heard him use words of endearment before! They sounded like swearing.

'And I don't know anything about your wallet.'

'What's it got to do with my wallet sweetheart?! You wanted my money!' Now he was talking in a low voice and almost spitting up into my face. He looked like a gangster. I had a sudden urge to laugh and closed my lips tightly before breathing in deeply.

'I wasn't....... I couldn't have done...... I can't read...' I began, speaking slowly although my heart was beating fast.

'Can't read? Do you expect me to believe that?

I tried to stay calm. There was silence for a moment.

'I'm reporting you to the management,' and he pulled a red string by his chair that made a buzzing noise. I knew what happened when you pulled those red cords, but I'd never seen it happen. I just stood there, waiting for someone to come. So this is how Nick had felt!

Not surprisingly, a member of staff had arrived anyway because of all the racket.

'What on earth is going on?' said Mrs Symonds

'She was reading about my money!'

'I was not!'

'She wants to see just how much money there is.'

'No I don't!'

'Calm down!' We both stopped talking. We were like a couple of toddlers squabbling over a bar of chocolate.

'Look,' I said. I was glad it was Mrs Symonds and she knew me. I picked up the piece of paper and pulled my hair behind my ears. 'He's accusing me of reading this......and I...... can't even see what's written on it.'

'Look, Mr. Darling, I think you're being a little paranoid.'

'What? You're going to believe her over me!' He was suddenly quiet. I could hear Mrs Symonds speaking in a low voice to him. Almost a whisper, but I heard what she was saying.

'Ha ha ha!' I mouthed to his reflection in the glass doors. I looked out at his straggly garden. It had started to sleet.

'I think you owe Louise an apology, Mr Darling.'

'Sorry, Louise.' He reminded me of when I used to have to apologise to Mark after we'd had a fight, or be sent to my room.

Mrs Symonds studied the piece of paper that he was holding and tutted. I frowned when I saw the distance from which she was able to read it.

'Mr. Darling,' she said deliberately. 'This is just a receipt.' She began to read. 'Mature Cheddar, one ninety five. Malted biscuits, one sixty'. At first I felt like sticking my tongue out at him, but he just seemed confused like a little child.

This time I'd had to talk about my eyes, and it had actually worked to my advantage. This was a strange new event, which made my heart pound.

It suddenly occurred to me that if he'd made a mistake about me then surely they would have to investigate the story about the wallet again. James started making little groaning noises. I'd never heard that before, he was usually so sure of himself .Maybe he was going mad.

'Sorry about that, Louise.' Mrs Symonds had come out into the corridor. 'I don't know what's got into him. He's not usually like this.'

'Maybe if he's confused about that, he might be about the wallet too,' I said,

'That could be possible....I don't see how though' she said thoughtfully. 'He's been strange lately, but there's still the fact that that wallet did disappear.'

Chapter 16

I met Nick as promised and we went to the little Cafe. I told him what had happened, and he seemed amazed and relieved.

'I told you he was lying Louise, didn't I?'

I smiled at him across the table.

School plodded on as usual through the rest of the term. My days were dominated with work and practice exams, and my evenings filled up with homework. There was so much of it that I thought I'd never really need to know about in the future. My friends all talked about how pointless it was to know about the periodic table and how to do simultaneous equations. It snowed a couple more times but only that watery slush that turns brown after a few hours. Some of the annoying boys at school thought it would be fun to make slushballs with stones in. I hated snow at school. It got into all the classrooms, and everywhere got cold and wet. It got into your shoes and froze your feet. And we weren't even allowed to wear trousers in winter. I wished Christmas would hurry up. I was one of those people who still got excited about Christmas and presents and singing. I liked being with my family. We seemed to get on better around Christmas.

I kept on seeing Nick, but never in school, because he was in a different form group and had different friends. We went to the harbour a lot and sat all huddled up together in our coats and gloves, watching the huge waves and hearing them crash. The sea was amazing when it was cold and windy. Most people only saw it on the warm days when the tourists were sunbathing on the beaches. It was strange how much noise it made. A massive, rhythmic crashing. All the tame little waves of the summer had grown up into huge monsters. Sometimes they came right over the harbour wall and splashed us and we messed about, dodging back and clutching our chip packets for warmth. The sky and sea were the same murky grey and it was hard to tell where one ended and the other began.

I went out a bit with the girls as well. Exams had started and I had to revise, even though everyone said that they weren't bothering, I'm sure they all did it secretly. I was trying to avoid Becky at school. There'd been loads of gossip about why she'd split up with David at the beginning but I hadn't listened to any of it. David had almost forgotten about her now, or so he said. He tried to convince me that he'd 'moved on'. We went to see a film in town and he came over to my house two or three times so we could revise together. That was what we said, anyway, but we usually ended up chatting about Primary School, or laughing at things we'd done in the past. Our relationship seemed to have changed in some subtle way, but I couldn't put my finger on how. I wanted to talk to him about Nick, and how I half-hoped he'd ask me officially to go out with him. Somehow the moment never seemed right.

Abby was going on a skiing holiday over Christmas. It was meant to be a treat for doing her exams and surviving the pressure. I was satisfied with the knowledge that I'd have a couple of weeks off in which I wouldn't have to do any work. Perhaps skiing felt a bit like ice skating. I might be good at that too. It had taken me months to get my courage back about skating, but I had decided not to give up. Naomi, Catherine and I went a few times. They enjoyed it but I had to admit to myself that I was secretly pleased that I was the best. We decided to make it quite a regular thing.

Craig and I were still in the same set for maths. He still made his rude comments and his witty remarks but, all that did for me was make me laugh on occasion. I'd thought that maybe after a while I'd get to fancying him again.

The mock exams happened just before the Christmas holidays. I was nervous even though the grades would mean nothing after the real things. My sight problem meant that I was allowed extra time. When I was younger and had to sit exams, I had refused to take it, as I'd have to remain in the hall on my own, and everybody would see me and ask why. Things had changed since then.

It was during the Physics exam that it happened. Only about half an hour of the test time had passed and I'd already run out of questions that I was capable of answering. I'd read the questions quite a few times, putting the emphasis on different words in the sentence in the hope that it would all become clear and of course it didn't. I squirmed uncomfortably in the seat, watching the bent backs and listening to the scratching of pens. I could imagine the big red 'U 'on the front of my paper and was trying not to care about it. When would I need physics in the future anyway? I gazed around the room. It was the hall where assemblies were held and it smelt of polish, especially at the beginning of term. My desk was rocking about all over the place and wobbly. I looked at the thick green curtains that hung on both sides of the stage at the front. I'd been in the school musical once. Only in the chorus. I hadn't had the guts to try for anything else and I didn't think I'd ever get a bigger part anyway. Besides, you had to read a tiny script straight off in rehearsals. I thought that maybe this year I'd do it. The script problem wasn't that scary was it? I could learn it at home before the first rehearsal. I looked up at the cloudy sky out of the windows at the top of the room. A seagull swooped by and cried loudly, breaking the stuffy silence. They must like the school. All the crumbs and half eaten sandwiches. Much easier than catching fish.

I stared at my watch, following the little shiny seconds hand as it ticked endlessly round. It isn't often that I actually noticed the sound of my watch, but now it was all I could hear through the thick silence of the room. I looked at the boy sitting beside me. He must be deep in thought. It wasn't fair.

'Erm, excuse me.' It was barely a whisper. Footsteps were coming towards me. The sound made me sit up. The invigilator! I must have looked guilty as hell.

'This desk is a bit close to the others. You weren't reading his answers?' He pointed to the person I'd been looking at who was now staring at me.

'No.'

'I'll have to report this to the head of science. I've been watching you for the past five minutes, and your eyes have been wandering all over the place.'

I sighed. 'Here we go again,' I thought

'Look, I couldn't have cheated even if I'd wanted to.' And butterflies came into my stomach as I explained.

He allowed me to continue to sit in silence. 'I don't see very well,' echoed around the huge hall. I wondered how many people had heard it.

Nick phoned me when I got home from school. He sounded excited.

'Guess what? Firtops just phoned me to apologise. They've found the wallet! They've finally realised it wasn't me.'

'That's fantastic.' I felt a huge surge of guilt at not believing him properly for all that time, before I'd come to realise it couldn't be true.

'I understand why you didn't totally believe me, Louise... But it's good that you trusted me enough for us to keep having a laugh.'

I felt a bit strange. I was glad he wasn't with me because a huge smile had spread across my face, and I couldn't stop it.

'What was the explanation? Where was it?'

'In one of his winter coats.'

'Then what was he talking about? Why did he lie....?'

'It's quite a story,' he said. 'Remember that fateful day when he accused you of wanting to steal his money? '

'Ellen's party?'

'Yeah! When he thought you were reading his Bank Statement. Apparently Mrs Symonds made a note of it in the Communications Book and the member of staff who followed on from her also found him doing lots of strange things.'

'Like what?'

'Oh, I don't know. It'd be even more fun if I did actually. But anyway, he felt really ill again.'

'Maybe he got drunk!' I was too excited to stop myself laughing. Nick chuckled too.

'Yeah, right! He had a really high temperature and felt so ill that they had to get a doctor to come and see him. Of course, they did lots of tests and one of them was his pee.'

I couldn't stop laughing now. It was great that Nick could joke about whatever it was.

'No, seriously!' he said. 'Apparently it's routine.'

'I hope I never get too ill then!'

'Well, they found out from the erm...urine test that he had an infection and that's what was making him grow gradually more confused. Apparently it's quite common in elderly people

'Really?'

'Yeah! It's mad isn't it? Like him I suppose'.

'A couple of days ago they had to get his winter coat out and that's where the wallet was! It all happened because his infection had literally made him go mad! He took antibiotics for the infection, which, I suppose, means to say he's sane again!

What an explanation! I wondered whether it had been the wrong thing to laugh. So that was why Mr Darling had been so confused at times, but not at others! The pang of pity I felt took me by surprise.

'I'm so glad I'm off the hook,' he said. 'You should have heard Mrs Symonds, she was so apologetic. Oh wow, it's started to snow again here! Has it there?'

I peered through the curtains at the miserable sky and saw the ground seemed to be turning a bit white, like sprinkles on top of a cake. It was proper snow this time. Hopefully it would stay for Christmas. I'd only ever seen a white Christmas on Christmas cards.

'Shall we meet up again sometime?'

'Yeah. Where shall we go? The café? The harbour?'

'I was thinking more along the lines of that restaurant in the town centre. You know, the one next to the church.'

'The Belfry?' I said in a stunned voice. It was the kind of place where you had to look smart, quite up-market. I wondered if he'd chosen it because he was going to ask me out. I'd been sort of hoping, hadn't I? We had such a good relationship. He was fun to be with, and good-looking with it! I'd decided weeks ago that I wasn't going to be the one to do the asking this time – not after the Craig fiasco.

'Yeah. I thought it might make a nice change.... For Christmas'

Chapter 17

I went to see Ellen that weekend. I felt a bit bad as I hadn't been for a while because of school. Her room had sprigs of holly and ivy all around it; on the TV and chest of drawers. I was sure that she enjoyed my visits as much as I did. I started to see her fairly regularly again and I would end up doing most of the talking these days, and she'd listen and laugh at my silly jokes. She didn't do much painting as she had in the summer which surprised me at first. Maybe she didn't do them in the winter.

'Hello Louise,' she said. 'I can't find inspiration to paint at the moment. It must be this gloomy weather. Everything is just grey isn't it?' The snow hadn't lasted for more than a day, much to my disappointment.

'Good about Nick, isn't it?' I said.

'Yes. It was a rather unusual explanation. It made a sensation around here, as I'm sure you can imagine. Edith has been in her element all week! James isn't well-liked, unfortunately'

'It's not surprising. He's horrible to everyone. It's his own fault.' I should have known better than to speak like that about anybody to Ellen.

'You don't know what he's been through in his lifetime, Louise. The hardships he's had to face. If people are unkind, isn't it best to be kind to them? They say the best way to learn is by example.'

And that was what got me thinking. She was right, as usual. I saw this vision of a young boy in some orphanage for disabled people, wasting away the days. Ellen thought he didn't have any relatives.

I gave Ellen a rose picture frame for Christmas to go with the daisy one, and in return she gave me a tiny box, saying I wasn't allowed to open it until Christmas Day. When I went over to deliver her present she was in a talkative mood, probably because of the 'festive spirit.' We had a great chat. She told me a little bit about her childhood, which I'd always been curious about. She hadn't been born disabled, as I'd always imagined.

She'd had TB when she was little and a complication of this had been something called osteomyelitis, an infection in her bones. She'd spent years in a hospital called a Sanatorium, miles away from her parents. They'd only been allowed to visit once a week. She could only just remember being able to walk, but had been six when her arm was amputated. Her father had been killed in the First World War and her mum hadn't been able to cope with Ellen at home.

'My mother was a wonderful person,' she said, smiling. Smiling!

'And so are you, Ellen'. But I didn't say it. I didn't need to. What an amazing personality she had, even though things had been so hard for her!

I went to The Belfry with Nick on Christmas Eve. It was lovely! The whole restaurant was decked out with candles and fir branches. Dead posh. Throughout the whole meal Nick seemed a bit embarrassed and withdrawn, and he insisted on paying at the end. I asked the waitress what the bill amount was and it was huge! He didn't ask me out, though. Was I disappointed? Perhaps he'd ask me next time we were together.

Ellen's present was a little model of a teddy bear that she'd made herself. It wore blue dungarees and a floppy hat. With it was a note saying that it was the first thing she'd ever made from clay when she had started doing art. I was honoured that she'd wanted to give it to me.

My aunt gave me some money, which I resolved to use for singing lessons. I was still jealous of Abby for having them so often. Nick gave me an enormous box of Thornton's chocolates and David gave me the CD I'd wanted. I was looking forward to earning some money of my own.

It didn't snow for Christmas. Gran came round for Christmas dinner. She wasn't a very ordinary grandma really. Mum's mum had always cuddled me when I was little and Mark and I would sit, one on each knee and she'd tell us stories. Dad's mum was a bit remote and a tad senile. Not recognising people. Perhaps it upset dad, although he didn't let on.

Later in the holiday I went to an ice disco with Georgina, Naomi and Catherine. It was great fun. I even managed to ice dance, to a tiny degree. The three of them showered me with praise. I felt so self-confident, which was a new feeling for me and I loved it. Things were changing. The tearful tantrums on my bed after 'breaking point' seemed to have decreased.

I always hated going back to school after the holidays, especially as now my GCSEs were so near. The teachers were already telling us to start revising. I was sure that anything I learnt now would be forgotten by the time the exams came in June.

It was a mild January, full of rain and watery sun. In February Valentine's Day made the school buzz with the usual gossip. Everyone – even those without a partner – hoped that perhaps they'd get something, but didn't dare believe that they would. Except the more popular ones among us, that is. Kate ripped open lots of cards on her desk and I don't suppose Craig did too badly either.

David gave me his usual type;

'Violets are blue
Roses are red
Be mine Louise
    Or I'll smash in your head.'

When I got home there was another card lying on the doormat. There was a big red heart on the front and simply "I love you" written in the middle. Nick phoned and said he wanted to see me that evening.

When I met him at Haslecombe harbour, after nagging for about half an hour for Mum to take me, he seemed all secretive. He was grinning too much. He smiled a lot anyway, but even I noticed that there was some kind of repressed excitement. I was pretty sure I knew what it was.

'Ok, Louise,' he said after we'd drunk a hot chocolate in the Cafe. I could tell he was really nervous. Not like himself at all. 'Louise, I've got something to ask you…' I knew what it was he was going to say. It was Valentine's Day. I'd just received an anonymous card. This was what I'd sort of been hoping for.

. 'Nick, stop.' I spoke before I'd had the chance to think. 'Please. Just don't say anything else.' He turned away and I felt uncomfortable and confused. Hadn't I been waiting for him to ask me officially to be his girlfriend? What was the matter with me?

We were standing so close to each other that I could see he'd turned pink and then pale. He mumbled a bit and got up to go, but I caught his hand.

'Nick, please. Please don't run away like they do in the films and never speak to me again. It would be such a waste.'

He sat down reluctantly, looking distressed. I felt really terrible and confused. I thought of changing my mind and saying, 'What were you going to ask,' to take that hurt look away. But I bit my tongue, my thoughts spinning.

We sat in silence, nibbling at biscuits, both feeling too awkward to say anything. I couldn't believe what had just happened. For the first time in my life I'd been about to be asked out, and I'd said 'no'. I had made a pact with Naomi and Catherine that if ever that happened I'd say 'yes' if I liked the person, just to give it a shot. How often I'd wished I had a boyfriend! And this was Nick!

'I'll phone you then, yeah?' he said, in a weak voice, and was brave enough to touch my arm. As he stood up I called behind him.

'Thanks Nick. It was a lovely thought. The card and all… it was really sweet.'

He turned back.

'Card? I haven't given it to you yet. I was going to give it to you this evening.'

Chapter 18

I felt dreadful for the next few days. I'd never disappointed anybody like that before and I couldn't work out how I was feeling myself. At least it gave me a chance to see David again. I hadn't seen him for a while. I didn't tell him about what had happened with Nick, but I did tell him about the Valentine's card and he seemed as mystified as I was. He didn't tease me as much as I thought he would, though. Perhaps his relationship with Becky had taught him something.

I started my singing lessons after half term and, although I'd never admit it to anybody, I was really pleased at how good my voice sounded. I even joined the school choir with Abby, and they seemed to know automatically that they needed to enlarge my sheets of music. There was a concert coming up in a couple of months and they were looking for soloists. David and Abby managed to persuade me to audition and, though obviously terrified at the thought of auditioning in the first place, I was accepted! How short a time ago I would never have dared. I loved singing. I even preferred it to ice-skating .I was recognising that there were some things I was good at. I hadn't decided what to sing yet. It was my choice, which made things more difficult in a way.

I told Ellen about it and she seemed enthusiastic.
'You'll have to come and see the concert,' I said. It sounded like a great idea. I don't suppose she went outside Firtops that much; it would be a nice treat. I wanted her to see how much I'd changed since the quiet little mouse that visited her during work experience.
'Maybe. Yes. Maybe.'

Perhaps I didn't allow myself to notice that things had changed with Ellen as well. She hadn't done a painting since before Christmas now and occasionally I'd find her sleeping in her chair.

Mrs Symonds phoned me one Friday afternoon in late March. I wondered why on earth she was phoning me. She never had before! I thought perhaps it was something to do with Mr Darling. Had he accused Nick of something else? Mrs Symonds didn't sound particularly happy. Had I done something wrong? Damaged something last time I went to see Ellen perhaps?

'Louise, how are you? We haven't spoken for a while.'

'Fine.'

'School going all right?'

'Yeah.' Actually I was completely bogged down. All the revision I was meant to be doing and wasn't! Had she just phoned for a friendly chat?

'It's Ellen, Louise,' she said this after a long pause. I breathed in sharply. I knew what she was going to say next. If I hung up the phone I'd never find out. It wouldn't be real.

'She definitely would have wanted me to contact you.' I noted the use of past tense.

'She had a stroke…. She was very old. 93.' I could tell Julie was used to breaking news like this. I suppose you have to be at a place like Firtops. I wondered what I should be feeling. And what I should say to her.

'I'm sorry.' Perhaps she thought I was crying.

'You can come to the funeral. It's at the local church. She definitely wanted you to be there. She never stopped talking about you.'

This news must have caused great upset at Firtops. Everybody had liked kind, quiet Ellen. It was strange. If Ellen wasn't here anymore, then where was she? I looked out of the window at the pouring rain. It was funny that it should be raining, I thought. It always rains on films when people die.

I spent the rest of the day in silence, feeling guilty because I wasn't in tears. I wanted to cry. This wasn't right. The odd feeling of not knowing where Ellen was shouted at me all afternoon. I kept thinking that maybe if I went to her flat she'd be there just the same, in her chair. Starting out on a new masterpiece, perhaps, or just watching the world. But she wouldn't be there and I wouldn't find her. Not in the day room or the laundry room or anywhere. I should have let Nick know, but I was nervous about phoning him. I thought of asking Mum to do it, but that would be too cowardly. When I eventually plucked up courage he already knew. He was going to the funeral too. We didn't have any conversation apart from that.

I thought of Ellen's little body all old and tired out. And that always happy voice that showed her ageless reality. I smiled. If all her God stuff was true then she was happy now. She was freed from that distorted shell.

I thought of all she'd taught me; about the paint incident. 'Just admit it Louise.' I could hear the running water laugh and her gentle voice. She'd be proud of me now. The tears came at last and I was relieved. Warm and comforting. I hoped that she could see me crying for her. I realised that there'd be no more visiting her and commenting on how well her paintings were doing; admiring her talent. As I thought of her I respected her more than ever.

I'd never been to a funeral before, so I wasn't sure what to expect. I didn't wear black. I thought it was the most inappropriate colour for Ellen. I went shopping and there was a long black dress. It was pretty, with little swirly patterns but I couldn't imagine Ellen liking it. Instead I wore the most colourful outfit in my wardrobe. Bright spring-time yellow blouse and a pale skirt. This was her spring time, I told myself. She'd gone to start a new, better life perhaps.

The day of the funeral was sunny, but cool and refreshing. Even the weather was doing what Ellen would have wanted. None of her paintings was of rain.

The church was really small and old. I'd only been in it once, for a carol concert at Primary School. I got to the door and joined the line of black-clad figures, walking in silence except for the crunch of our feet and the rumble of wheelchairs on the gravel. Sniffs told me that some were crying. I thought that perhaps it was disrespectful that I wasn't.

We filed in and sat on the wooden pews. Although there were daffodils all over the church, I felt miserable and out of place. I should be wearing black as well. My bright clothes looked garish and wrong. I sat down uncomfortably next to Nick, who was wearing a suit and had made himself all smart. I wanted to hide, or get a big black shawl to drape over myself. Julia had guided us to a pew right at the front of the church. She didn't say anything, but she knew and I knew that I should be sitting there.

The vicar started the service and I could hear sniffs around me. I really wanted to cry too, but again the tears wouldn't come. How much better a life she could have had! Imagine being an outcast from society because of a disability. Did I really appreciate how lucky I was? I imagined the hell she must have been through when she was my age. Nobody was there to care about her and help her to get over it.

We sang hymns that I didn't know and I was relieved because I was too choked to make a sound. No more going round to her flat for a chat. I hoped everyone here realised how amazing she was. That there was nothing nasty about this seemingly unimportant woman. What if she wasn't in her heaven, having the wonderful life that I'd imagined. What then? But really she'd had a wonderful and fulfilling life here hadn't she? Of course she had!

I looked at the tiles on the floor underneath my polished shoes, when suddenly I saw that the bright sun had come out from behind a cloud and was pouring through the big stained glass window in a blaze of colour, right over Ellen's coffin. Red, blue, green and yellow, highlighting the displays of daffodils. I couldn't see out through it, yet it enhanced the sunlight coming in.

For some reason I thought of my eyes.

And then I cried freely with everyone around me, but I wasn't upset exactly. The colour and the light made me think that wherever Ellen was, she must be OK. We sang her favourite hymn, *'How Great Thou Art'* and I picked up the programme in front of me, expecting to have to pretend to mouth the words, but it was in large print, especially for me, just as she would have wanted and my voice came out through the tears, along with those of all her friends.

After it was all over, we went back to Firtops. I asked Nick if he was coming, but he had to get back home. Everyone had some kind of memory about Ellen and there were all happy stories. When they had all gone, Mrs Symonds took me aside. We went to her office where a flat, rectangular parcel stood by the desk and she picked it up.

'She wanted you to have this.'

I put the picture on my wall in pride of place. Just above my bed where the notice board used to be, so that I'd see it whenever I walked into the room. It would always remind me of her. It would remind me to 'be strong' like she'd said and admit about my eyes. I looked especially at the shades of yellows in the daffodils and then drank in the whole scene. A field full of them where a bright sun hung in a springtime blue sky.

Chapter 19

Even though at least a month had passed since Valentine's Day, I still felt uncomfortable round Nick. We'd hardly seen each other except for at the funeral, and that wasn't exactly a social event. I wondered how he was feeling. I'd made the right decision, though. For some reason I couldn't see myself as his girlfriend. I didn't quite know why.

I was pleased when he phoned me one evening. Hopefully this was a step towards us being friends again.

'About Valentine's day.' I'd guessed he would bring it up sooner or later.

'I'm sorry I upset you, Nick. You're one of my best friends,' I said quickly.

'You didn't upset me! Look, Louise, I really like you, and I still want to be your friend. I hope you understand.'

'Course I do!'

'I should have realised right from the start that David's the one for you. He was joking… wasn't he?

'You are having a laugh?

'No! You're always talking about him when we're together! It's so obvious!'

'That's because he's my friend.'

'And you go on about what's her name, er, Naomi, all the time as well then do you? I don't think so!'

'But David and I are best friends. We've known each other since we were little kids. You think that he and I should go out?'

He gave a loud laugh.

'It's up to you what you SHOULD do. I just agree with half the school! Anyway I really will be in touch soon. I'll try to smile when I see you in school.' He laughed as he said goodbye.

Now I really was confused. Why would Nick want to wind me up? Had he sent me that card for a joke? David was definitely the sort to help me solve the mystery, not be the root cause of it.

So how come, when I was lying in bed that night, thoughts of David and me going out were still plaguing me? Because it was such a weird idea? I thought about all the things we'd done together. Ever since we were really small. All the time I'd spent with him, all the secrets we'd shared. How, after a few days, I felt that I had to phone him if we hadn't seen each other. Even during all that time I'd spent with Nick. And how bad I'd felt about neglecting David over that patch.

I let myself imagine going out with David. Just to make sure that Nick was wrong, just to put a stop to all of these stupid thoughts. Why did it seem right? What was I thinking of?

I'd been so pleased when he'd split up with Becky, hadn't I? But that was because I didn't like her, and I thought she was wrong for David, wasn't it? Who did I think was right for him then? I laughed out loud at everything that was going through my head. The noise was startling through the silence.

As the hours went by, I still couldn't sleep. It was about 1 in the morning and I got it. Finally after all this time, I got it! It was David! And somebody else had had to point it out for me.

I felt great for a little while. Thinking of how good it would be after our relationship changed, forgetting that half the school might be wrong. It had been known in the past. All those rumours that Thomas Jackson in the sixth form was in line to be a pop singer had been a load of nonsense. David might think the idea was as stupid as I had at first. What if he turned me down? Things would change forever. I had to stop thinking about it to prevent the feeling from getting stronger. I decided never to let the thought pop into my mind again. I'd had plenty of practice at that.

I spent long hours with my singing teacher, practising for the concert, which was in a couple of weeks. I'd never sung alone, in public before. Only in the shower or in front of the mirror.

However hard I tried, I couldn't stop thinking about David. Whenever we were together, the feeling that I wanted more than just friendship was there. I had to stop it. He'd never see me in the same way again if he found out.

Nick and I had resumed a sort of friendship, which I was pleased about. I'd heard that he was seeing a lot of a girl in the year below, and hoped that something would come of it. David and I still spent the majority of our free time together. Not that there was much. I had finally persuaded myself to revise and the stress was building up. In maths I felt sure I hadn't covered half the topics in the first place. I told myself that I wouldn't be upset about my science grade.

All this work gave me hardly any time to think about my eyes. Things seemed to be going back to the way they had been when I was little, and feeling different hadn't been an issue. Sometimes, believe it or not, I even forgot. At other times, like the occasional sleepover with my friends, when they all started discussing what kind of cars they were going to buy when they were 17 those old feelings would come again. They'd go on about how dependant they were on their parents at the moment, and how much better things would be when they weren't restricted to the buses and trains. I decided not to let it get me down. I couldn't blame them for being honest around me.

The future had started to play realistically on my mind. It wasn't that far away now. I agreed to have the mobility training that I'd been so cross about last year. They gave me another telescope to replace the one I'd rejected. I still wasn't comfortable with going out and using it. It brought back some of the old feelings. The blushing and humiliation and frustration. And sometimes I'd clench my fists and wonder why I couldn't just get around naturally, like everybody else.

The concert went well. I don't think I'd ever been so nervous before. Waiting for my turn under the stage lights of the school hall, I almost felt that I couldn't do it. Maybe if I ran away it would be OK. The first few notes were a bit shaky, but once I got going I kind of forgot that anybody was watching me. That might sound like a cliché, but it was true. I imagined I was in that little room with just my singing teacher. I loved it when the audience applauded. Nobody had ever clapped exclusively for me before except at my birthday parties or at prize-giving. This was something I was definitely going to do again! I resolved that day I was going to take my lessons more seriously and practise a bit harder.

Afterwards I was surprised at the amount of congratulation I got from everybody – even from people I didn't know. One girl came up to me, carrying a flute. She was wearing a sparkly blue top. I recognised her as the one who had done a fantastic flute solo.

'You were really good,' I told her.

'Thanks, it's for my GCSE. You were great too.'

It was Becky Myres! I hadn't seen her and heard her voice for so long that I'd forgotten how to recognise her.

'Do you mind if I ask you something, Louise?' she said after a pause. I don't think I'd spoken to her since she'd split up with David. I had no reason to, we weren't really friends. She didn't sit next to David any more in History.

'Go on.'

'David. Are you going out with him yet?'

'What?' Had I let it slip to somebody by mistake? Had she read my mind?

'Oh… perhaps I shouldn't have said anything.'

'What? What do you mean?'

'I just thought somebody should tell you, that's all.'

'Tell me what?'

'You must be so unobservant!' I blushed before realising that she didn't mean literally. 'I think everybody knows that he fancies you, except you!'

'You what?'

'You really haven't seen it have you? And you spend so much time with him. It's a good job I'm telling you now, or you'd never have worked it out.' Was she saying I was thick?'

'I don't understand. You're saying he fancies me?!'

I lowered my voice as I noticed that a few people were turning round.

I pretended to look alarmed, but underneath I sincerely hoped that she was saying that.

'Only for ever! That's why we split up; because he kept going on about you all the time! And that was what? Months ago!'

'He never told me anything.'

'He made me promise not to as well. Didn't want to 'ruin your friendship'. He's so sweet. That's why I went out with him, but it seems he was already taken.'

I wanted to ask her more. Like was she sure. But she'd already said goodbye and gone.

***

Chapter 20

David and I couldn't believe how much time we'd wasted. It wasn't a week before we were 'official.' The whole thing seemed unreal.

I'd had to talk to a few people first, just to check it was all true and that Becky wasn't just trying to stitch me up. She hardly knew me after all. But Nick had told me the same thing hadn't he? Everybody seemed to have the same suspicion, so I took the plunge one Saturday afternoon. We were having a light-hearted conversation about how they put the caramel into chocolate bars. This was so silly. We both felt the same way about each other, but were doing nothing. How many would-be relationships never happened because of that?

We were sitting at the table in our living room. Everyone was out, thank goodness. I could never have had this conversation with Mark anywhere in the vicinity.

'David,' I said. I suddenly had his full attention. He must have known something out of the ordinary was coming, by his unusually timid response.

'What have I done?' I smiled through my nerves. He had such a fun sense of humour! But what if all my friends had got it wrong? I couldn't go back now.

'At the concert, I was speaking to Becky.'

'Becky? Why? Are you mates now or something?'

'She told me something.'

'Sounds ominous.'

'About you.'

'Sounds very ominous. You know, I thought we were back on good terms now. She's got another boyfriend.'

'Never mind about her. She said something about you….'

I was close enough to read the horror in his expression. He knew what I was talking about, but made a joke instead.

'Hey, she didn't tell you I was rubbish did she? It's not true, Louise… don't believe it.' He was trying to make me laugh, but I knew that if I did we'd go off the point and I'd never be able to say what I wanted to.

'She said that you fancied me.' He looked away. I felt like a teacher telling off a child. Maybe I'd gone about this the wrong way. Perhaps I should have confessed to liking him first. But it was out in the open now.

He didn't speak for ages.

'Because if it is,' I began, heart pounding. I'm not a natural romantic. 'Don't worry.'

'Why?… I'll kill her. She had no right to say that!'

'It's Ok… because…because… I feel the same.'

He turned his head back to face me, then looked away again.

'You don't have to say that to make me feel better.'

'So it's true then? Becky was right?'

'That Valentine. It was from me. But I didn't want you to find out, because I thought you were going to go out with Nick.'

'He was the one that made me understand.'

He looked at me again, finally realising that I was telling the truth.

'We're so slow aren't we?' I said. 'We've been friends forever, and it took us until now to work it out!

He smiled and answered me with a kiss. It felt strange at first. This was David! But somehow, I knew it was right.

The weeks that followed were amazing. Nobody seemed surprised to hear our news. I'd always spent a lot of time with David, but now I spent even more. Naomi, Georgina, Catherine and Abby made sure that I didn't completely lose touch with the real world, however. We would go ice skating together quite often and we all enjoyed it.

It took ages for it to get hot that summer. There would be loads of days when it was too hot to wear a jacket but too cold to wear just a T shirt. The heat was definitely on in school, however. My brain felt as though it might burst from all the facts I was trying to cram into it. I wondered how many I'd actually manage to trap inside it for the exams.

I had to keep telling myself that it really didn't matter if I didn't do too well. The teachers were making that difficult, as they made it seem like we were guaranteed a job sweeping the streets if we got less than a 'C' for anything. I'd decided that I'd go to the sixth form of the school next year, along with most of the rest of my friends, except Catherine, who was going to Haslecombe College instead.

To get some money I spent my spare hours helping out at Firtops. They all knew me well there now, and seemed to like me. Most of the time I was cleaning, but I didn't mind that. I had time to talk to people, which I enjoyed. An elderly couple was now living in Ellen's old flat. It felt weird at first. Somebody else exactly where she had been, but I soon got to like them. The man was blind and had a beautiful black guide dog. I spent lots of time putting myself in his shoes and realising how fortunate I was. But he was happy and incredibly independent.

There were loads of leavers' events at the end of the year, before the start of the exams. I could hardly believe that I'd nearly finished compulsory education for good.

There was a ball to be held at The White Horse Hotel in Haslecombe, which was the talk of all the girls in year 11. We got formal dresses and the boys would wear suits. David and I were going as a couple. David looked brilliant in a suit. I'd never seen him look like that before, and I liked it. I bought a long dark-blue dress that I'd saved up for with my money from work. Perhaps I even looked pretty.

It was a wonderful night. The first proper event I'd been to with David. We danced together and loads of my single friends smiled as they passed us. I was really happy, temporarily forgetting the dreaded exams that were to come in a couple of weeks. Although I'd been stressed-out lately, I hadn't been really upset about anything for a while. I'd forgotten when the last breaking point and temper tantrum had happened.

'You look great, Louise!' It was Nick!

'I don't think you know Jo, do you?' I looked up as he grabbed the hand of a pretty blonde girl, and pulled her towards him.

'Hello'.

'Hi!'

She seemed really happy like me.

David broke away from me after the next song to go and get a drink. I went to sit down at the side, and found myself next to a girl in a dark purple dress – really attractive. I wished I had a figure like that. We started chatting. I'd come out of myself lately and I was more willing to talk to people I didn't know very well.

'Oh, I know you, you're Louise Jordan! You're going out with someone called David aren't you?' I hadn't known it was that public!

'Where's he gone?'

'Over to the bar to get a drink.'

'Which one is he?' she said, studying the numerous men around the bar.

'I'm afraid I couldn't tell you unless I went right up to stare at all their faces,' I said, laughing. 'I can't see very well.'

THE END